# EVERYTHING
## SHE DOES IS
### *Magic*

# EVERYTHING
## SHE DOES IS
# *Magic*

### BRIDGET
### MORRISSEY

**DELACORTE
ROMANCE**

Delacorte Romance
An imprint of Random House Children's Books
A division of Penguin Random House LLC
1745 Broadway, New York, NY 10019
penguinrandomhouse.com
GetUnderlined.com

Editor: Hannah Hill
Cover Designer: Casey Moses
Interior Designer: Ken Crossland
Production Editor: Colleen Fellingham
Managing Editor: Tamar Schwartz
Production Manager: Shameiza Ally

Library of Congress Cataloging-in-Publication Data is available upon request.
ISBN 978-0-593-89843-7 (trade) — ISBN 978-0-593-89844-4 (ebook)

The text of this book is set in 10-point Frutiger Serif LT Pro.

Manufactured in the United States of America
2nd Printing

The authorized representative in the EU for product safety and compliance
is Penguin Random House Ireland, Morrison Chambers, 32 Nassau Street,
Dublin D02 YH68, Ireland, https://eu-contact.penguin.ie.

This one is for the Marnie to my Sophie, and the Fran to my Jet, and the Diana to my Cassie, and every other member of my coven who doesn't have a fictional witch counterpart.

# 26 Days Until Halloween

# 1

## DARCY

"As the legend goes, on Halloween night, in the thick of the for-est, where the trees make the shape of a Trinity knot and when the clock hovers between eleven and twelve, you can look up in the clearing and see a witch on her broomstick."

The tourists watch me with intense interest, tracking my every flick and flourish.

"Only the luckiest among us are privileged with this view," I continue, dropping my voice into the lowest part of my register. "The moon must be full, or the witch won't be visible. Not to human eyes, at least. But she's always there, every Hallows' Eve, sprinkling another year of good fortune atop our little town of Fableview."

Scattered flecks of golden glitter shimmer out of my hands and into the air. I do a dramatic swoosh with my cape, throw-ing it over the blank art canvas beside me. When the cape settles again at my ankles, the canvas has been transformed. There is now a painting of a witch flying over the forest, sprinkling magic dust onto the trees, exactly as I described her. She looks like me—long black cape covering her body, low-heeled boots on her feet, and blond waves flowing out from beneath her pointy hat.

My audience applauds as I strum my fingers together in delight, pretending this transformation is the work of my magical powers, not a practical stunt my parents taught me when I started teaching some of the art classes here at Pam's Paints.

The easel is spring-loaded. When my cape covers it, I knock off the blank canvas and press a button to bring up the finished art piece. If anyone listens closely, they can hear the *sproing* of the completed painting's appearance. It's not fancy, and it's not supposed to be. We rely on simple practical effects that can be executed multiple times a month.

Pam's Paints sits smack-dab in the middle of Fableview Boulevard—a cobblestoned road that's used less for driving and more for outdoor festivals and parades. Tourists come here because they want to experience a piece of our town's charm. Fableview is known for our commitment to all things mystical, particularly witches. Saying "real witches" live here is a huge part of our town's lore. That's what draws tourists to us every October, and it's why our local businesses commit to Halloween at the level we do.

And sure, my fellow residents love to tell tales of things that have happened here that might seem unexplainable, maybe even magical. I've been known to share a few of these stories myself when they help set the right mood for the tourists. I'll talk about the summer afternoon a strange fog settled over the boulevard for almost an hour and then evaporated. Or the time a murder of crows gathered along the power line at exactly midnight and started to sing. Not caw but *sing*.

These stories make our town feel special. They make tourists want to visit again and again. But when it comes down to it, I know there's a logical explanation behind these occurrences, even when I haven't yet figured out what it is. Just like with me and this painting—there's *always* a catch.

Not everyone in Fableview is a skeptic. Some residents really believe our town has witches. Probably because it's what they've grown up hearing, and every corner of Fableview looks like a place a "real witch" might want to live.

The truth is, that witchy, whimsical feeling is because of my parents and me. We're in charge of decorating the town square every fall. We host the Halloween paint nights and themed events throughout October. We encourage everyone to wear costumes all month long. *We* make the real magic around here.

"Tonight we pay honor to this witch of good fortune, known to us as Darcy," I say to my painters, winking.

Darcy is *my* name. It's always more fun to make them think that I'm the witch I speak of, even though it doesn't make any sense. *Sense is the enemy of wonder*, as my dad is so fond of reminding me. My grandma created the original version of this painting over forty-five years ago. At the time, the witch in the painting was named and modeled after her. Then it was modeled after my mom. It still is anytime she teaches this particular class. Some tourists go their whole lives believing a witch named Pam blesses our town each Hallows' Eve.

*Pam.*

Just as the classic legends foretold.

"With every stroke of our brushes, we paint her as she wants to be remembered—as a beacon of hope and a protector of Fableview," I finish.

For as ridiculous as these tall tales are, the magic is in the making. It doesn't matter if what I say isn't true. My enjoyment is real. And so is our commitment to making the entire month of October an unforgettable spectacle for everyone who comes through our town.

My best friend, Grace, heads my way, sticking out her elbow to knock over a can full of paintbrushes. "Anya Doyle just walked by *again*," she hisses through her teeth, gesturing for me to bend down and clean up the mess with her. "That's the fourth time in the last ten minutes."

"Maybe she's enjoying an evening stroll on the boulevard?" I say. "Lost in the beauty of the moment? I did put up new twinkle lights yesterday."

"Does Anya Doyle seem like the type of girl who gets lost in the beauty of the moment?" Grace asks. The question isn't for me. It's a setup for her to answer, so I let the silence swell until she finishes her thought. "Of course not. She's *sinister*. I think she's a witch. With *dark* magic."

"Please," I say. "You think everyone might be a witch. You told me last month you thought I was a witch because I passed that pop quiz in math."

"And I stand by that. Understanding math is magical. But this is different. Anya's a real witch."

"Okay, then why am I the one in the pointy hat and cloak?" She rolls her eyes.

Grace Manalo is the most dramatic person I have ever known. That's a high bar to clear in a town where every resident treats October like a monthlong costume contest complete with daily whimsical side quests. But Grace is a lot like her current makeup—bold in a way that few other people would ever attempt, much less pull off. She is the living embodiment of lavender glitter eye shadow and iridescent lip gloss. She started working at Pam's Paints with me last year. While she doesn't have a natural knack for the artistic element of the job like I do, she's very good at capturing the *vibe*. She even got herself a complementary costume for our witchy paint nights.

A person who knows her less might assume she'd want to *also* be a witch, but Grace fears us dressing alike the way other people fear snakes or the dark. Her individuality complex is so severe that most nights before school, she sends me a picture of her outfit for the following day. She wants to be sure we're not wearing the same thing, as if I've ever once owned a pair of hand-bleached oversized jeans and thought to pair them with a baby doll tee covered in pictures of lizards.

Tonight she is costumed as a basset hound, and she's created an entire backstory around it. Basset hounds have an incredible sense of smell, and in Grace's head canon, the dog is the scout who guides the witch to the Trinity knot, capable of recognizing the correct location by the smell of the tree sap. A few weeks ago, Grace and I collaborated on a version of the witch painting that featured the dog. We wanted to teach it that way tonight, but my mom couldn't bring herself to commit to the change.

"She lives with her aunt in that creepy purple Victorian house on Maple Lane," Grace says. "You can't tell me that's not a witch's house."

"Everything here looks that way," I say.

"Yeah, but her aunt stalks around town the same way Anya does." Grace brushes her flopping dog ears out of her face with a heaving sigh, the fluffy fabric sticking to the gloss on her lips. "I wouldn't be surprised if they're the ones who used their magic to unleash the toads in the bookstore."

"That was a prank, not an act of magic." I stand up and return the brushes to the shelf. "We'll start with painting our canvases a deep blue," I announce to the class, showing them which acrylic to select, then squeezing it onto my palette. "Go ahead and grab the big brush that's sitting next to your canvas. We're going to make long, broad strokes. Just like this."

A lot of our customers are adults. In every other area of my life, they are supposed to be the ones teaching me. But here I get to lead. They don't know I'm seventeen, or if they do, no one makes a fuss about it. Not when they get to leave with their own Fableview painting that may or may not be of me, the supposed witch of good fortune, keeping our town prosperous and safe all year long.

*This* is what I will miss the most if I ever get the chance to actually leave Fableview—the permission to be powerful without any other box needing to be checked.

"Anya's looking in the window right now," Grace tells me as she grins at our audience with an expression that's giving *this building is on fire* more than *so excited to help you make your one-of-a-kind Fableview souvenir.*

My eyes stay on my canvas as I drag my paintbrush back and forth. "What's she doing?"

"She's looking at you," Grace tells me.

"No she's not. Or maybe she's familiar with the long-forgotten witch and basset hound legend, and she can't believe we're finally bringing it the representation it deserves."

"Do something specific," Grace commands.

"No."

Grace taps my painting hand. "I need to track her eye movements."

Despite my best interests, there has always been something about Grace that pushes me to be bolder. If she can move through the world as a glitter-encrusted basset hound who is known for being obsessed with reptiles, I can dance like no one's watching or whatever.

"*Yahtzee!*" I shout, tossing my hands up into triumphant fists as I take a large, lunging step to the right.

Our painters give a collective gasp of surprise. Grace startles like I've thrown something. Refusing to explain myself, I continue to paint the blue background until Grace tells me if the plan worked. This is not my burden to bear.

"Okay, she's definitely watching you," Grace confirms. A hot lash of adrenaline singes my core. "What if she's, like, obsessed with you?"

"Anya Doyle is *not* obsessed with me," I challenge as another lash, faster than the last one, almost knocks me over with its intensity.

"Yeah," Grace says. "You're right."

It doesn't bother me that Grace agrees, despite having pitched the idea exactly two seconds ago. Whatever makes the hairs prick up on the back of my neck must be an unrelated phenomenon.

"It's probably nice to have no one in this town really know you. I'd be a brooding mystery too if anyone who lives here would let me," I say.

"No you wouldn't."

"Okay, no, I have no idea how to brood, and I'd probably be

very bad at it, but it would be cool to make a single decision about my life that didn't have to get run by the Fableview Fall Planning Committee." Redirecting my attention to my painters, I raise my voice to the clear, confident tone I've grown accustomed to using in this setting. "We're not chasing perfection here. A good painting is about *feeling*. Give the blue whatever emotion you want it to possess. After all, art is its own form of magic. No matter how closely you follow our design, this painting will still be your own original creation."

"Have you ever spoken to her?" Grace asks, not letting the whole Anya thing go despite my attempt to redirect her to the job we are supposed to be doing together.

"When she moved here last year, Madame Poncik sat her behind me in French," I whisper. "On her first day, I turned around and said, 'Anya's a really cool name.' She just nodded. Didn't say anything back. So I tried again the next day. I asked her how she was liking Fableview. And she didn't answer me."

This makes Grace laugh. It comes out like a bark, which is fitting, considering her costume. "See?" she says. "Sinister."

"I think she's just shy," I challenge, even though at the time, I took great offense at Anya's silence.

We hadn't had anyone new join our grade in years. Though we get many tourists in Fableview, we don't get many new residents. Anya's presence would've been exciting to me no matter what. But she seemed so *interesting*. Completely unlike anyone else in our class. She was closed off, as anyone probably would be when moving to a place as tight-knit as Fableview, but she also seemed very herself. She wore all black—down to a thin velvet choker on her neck and stacks of black bracelets made of crystals and uniquely coiled metals—in a way that didn't feel like a performance or a costume. She carried around tattered hardcover books that were so old they didn't have dust jackets on them, just titles printed in small gold fonts. I couldn't get a close enough look at any of them to know what they were. The bag she carried with her everywhere had buttons on it with the names of bands I'd never heard of. When I went home and played their music, it was all melancholic and deep, which was exactly how I imagined Anya herself would be.

I wanted to know her, but she did *not* want to know me back.

Whenever I turn around to pass her an assignment or get paired with her to go over a worksheet, I still try to get her to meet my eye. Ask me a question. Anything. But she won't. Which is what makes it even stranger that she's standing outside my parents' art shop, supposedly looking at me.

"We've spoken since that first day, I'll have you know," I tell Grace.

"Yeah, *in* French," Grace says.

She happens to be correct, so I continue painting, lips pursed.

Grace folds her arms, fully aware she's got me clocked. "All I'm saying is that whatever she wants, it must be a bad thing, or she'd have come inside already. She might even hate you."

"Then we better hope she stays outside," I say.

# 2

# ANYA

When Emily Dickinson wrote that if your nerve denies you, you need to go above your nerve, she must have known someone like Darcy Keller would someday exist and I would have to find the strength to talk to her.

Darcy Keller attracts attention the way rainbows do after storms. It's impossible to be in her presence and not marvel at her. For one, she smiles with all her teeth, right back to the molars. It's wide-open, inviting. Enveloping. I'm not sure how her friend Grace can stand to hold dozens of conversations with her every single day. Grace must forget her train of thought all the time, especially when Darcy laughs so hard that she has to put a hand on Grace's arm to steady herself.

And Darcy's *eyes*. They are a calcite kind of green, so bright they're almost translucent. She squints them whenever someone speaks to her, like she's trying to climb into the words and experience whatever the other person is saying. It's not a surprise to learn she's as confident in her art as she is everywhere else.

She manages to load her brush with the exact amount of paint needed to make an unbroken stroke across her entire canvas.

Staring at her from outside the window at Pam's Paints is not what I've come here to do, but it's all I'm capable of at the moment.

Grace has given me more than one menacing glare. It's turned into an actual, genuine scowl now, like she's a real guard dog. Although I don't think basset hounds are known for being intimidating. Not that Grace is what's deterring me. My presence is never an exciting development anywhere in this town. But I don't usually have so much to lose by showing up somewhere.

I back away from the window again.

There is too much energy inside me. Adrenaline, pressure, butterflies. I can't talk to Darcy until I manage to contain at least one of these feelings.

I squat down to examine one of the flower beds along Fable-view Boulevard. This one is filled with asters. They're sweet-looking flowers, with delicate purple petals and sunny yellow centers. Most of them are thriving. There are a few near the edge that have been stepped on or rolled over from the foot traffic on the boulevard. Not dead, but close to it.

Cupping one of the damaged flowers in my hand, I take a focused inhale, conjuring up the image of a sky awash with in-finite gray. Gentle fists of water drumming against a window. Sulfuric sweetness perfuming the air.

A new heartbeat begins to pulse through me—the undeni-able, jittering thrum of magic—traveling out through my breath and into the aster. It's a current not unlike electricity, with me as the conduit, using the energy to revive the deadened petals inside my palm. The first spark of power always makes me feel filled to the brim with purpose and possibility.

*We're so excited!*

My mother's words cloud my focus, snapping the connection to my power. Huffing out a breath, I release my first attempt at mending this flower.

All good magic comes from breathing. Inhale intentions, exhale actions. Steady as a hiss of steam, constant as a moving train. Let the breath mold the mind and move the magic through the body.

I breathe in again, returning to the image of rain, letting it wash over the flower. Over me.

*We have to meet her!*

I've never touched a socket with a wet hand, but it must be similar to this, the way my own power zaps through me, sharp and jagged and wrong.

*We're booking an early flight so we can spend Halloween with you and her before your big birthday! See you at the end of the month!*

"Shit!" I exclaim, wincing. Where the aster once lived there is now ash falling from my hand.

Great. I have killed the flower I meant to mend.

This was a mistake. Coming here to Pam's Paints. Living in Fableview at all. It has been nothing short of a colossal misstep, and it will result in my being the first witch in my bloodline to fail my initiation into our coven next month.

My gift has become a weighted vest, burdening everything I do. My magical instinct is to mend things, but there's so much that's broken in the world, and there are too many people who want me to fix it. I can never do enough.

The crunch of leaves beneath my feet provides a soothing soundtrack to my renewed pacing. I have loved October in many places. It is in my bloodline to do so. I'm named after the goddess Áine, who is known for bringing love, protection, and prosperity to Ireland. In some ways, she is nature itself, and I am an extension of that. It's a lot to live up to, and my family doesn't ever let me forget it. Between my storied name and my rare magical gift, it's impossible to escape the pressure. Everyone who knows what I can do needs something from me. I'm the one who mends tattered clothing, patches holes in walls, revives dying plants. I repair what others cannot, and all it's done is turn my own life into a mess.

"You have the potential to be the most powerful witch this coven has seen in centuries," my Uncle Edward once told me. "If only you were more enjoyable to be around."

He'd muttered that last part to himself, but I'd heard him. He was frustrated with me for once again sitting quietly through one of his lectures on our family history. He wasn't the first to mistake my silence for disinterest, but he was the loudest about it, thinking that if he made enough sly comments on the subject, I would transform into a social butterfly through the strength of his annoyance. I was twelve years old at the time, and my life was already hard, moving from family member to family member to hone my powers and learn our coven's ways, never staying in one place long enough to get comfortable.

I'd thought the easiest thing to do would be to give it all up, so I'd asked Uncle Edward what would happen if a witch failed to join our coven. He'd told me, "We'd use a very old spell in the family grimoire, and we'd strip that person of their power. No one in the family would ever speak to them again. It would be a very taxing process for everyone. It's only happened once, centuries ago. I would tell you more, but there isn't more to say. We don't know what came of her after the family banished her."

You don't want that, do you? So why don't you start acting a little nicer?"

It scared me so much that I still have nightmares to this day, imagining my entire family locking hands around me, chanting some Doyle spell in Gaelic as they pull my powers out of me like steam hissing from a teapot, until my gift has evaporated into nothing and they've left me lying on the ground to fend for myself.

Returning to the flowers, I squat down again, touching the asters that remain. "I'm sorry, I only meant to fix your friend," I whisper.

No matter what I do, that phone call with my parents can't be erased from my memory. Nearly a year's worth of lies all came to a head with a five-word sentence, spoken without consideration.

*Her last name is Keller.*

For months my mom and dad had been thrilled to hear about my new best friend, Darcy. Everyone in the family thinks I'm too intense for my own good. While that's usually a frustration, it's made telling this lie much easier, because my parents have been so happy I'm giving them any information at all that they haven't wanted to ruin the moment by asking too many questions, knowing that with one wrong word, I might stop talking altogether.

At no point had I been consciously withholding Darcy's last name. It just hadn't come up. Probably because this lie has been such a delicate dance, I spend most of my calls with my parents talking around it as much as possible. But tonight I said "Keller," and my mother shrieked so loudly, I dropped my phone.

"How wonderful! That's Pam Keller's daughter!" she shouted, audible even from the space between the couch cushions. "I can't believe I didn't put it together with Darcy's first name. It's just been so long since I've been to Fableview. But I know her parents. And her grandmother protected yours. Oh, this is incredible. I always knew Fableview would be the place where you finally figured it all out. I bet Aunt Cal is just as thrilled as we are."

Aunt Cal is my guardian here, chosen as my final mentor because she has the least patience for young children. She didn't want to work with me until after I turned seventeen. My mom assured me that Cal and Fableview would make me fall completely in love with my magic.

Cal hasn't spoken to me out loud in six weeks. Through a note she scribbled onto handmade paper, written in a cursive so close to chicken scratch I had to use my mending magic to turn it into something legible, she wrote, *I am exploring new depths of my magic through limiting access to my senses. I will no longer be using my voice to communicate. There are pizzas in the freezer. Do not use my eggs.*

*Okay*, I'd written back.

I knew this Darcy Keller lie would one day come back to haunt me. I had hoped to make at least one actual friend before that happened.

But here I am, guilty, friendless, hovering around the entrance to Pam's Paints and burning flowers instead of going inside to ask Darcy to come to a dinner with my parents at the end of the month. The usual activity of a brand-new acquaintance. No pressure at all.

*Oh, and, by the way, I'm a witch and I need to bring a mortal friend to my coven initiation in November. Are you free?*

I'm very sorry, Emily Dickinson, but my nerve will always deny me.

And soon my family will too.

# 3

# DARCY

"Howdy, painters!" My dad jogs down the stairs that separate the art shop from our condo above it.

My mom follows behind him. "Welcome to witchy paint night!"

My parents rarely let me teach a class without making at least one appearance. Tonight my mom is dressed as Sandy from *Grease*. Not the bodysuit-wearing, hair-teased Sandy from the end of the movie, but the poodle-skirt-and-cardigan one from the beginning. My dad is dressed as Rick Moranis's character from the original *Ghostbusters*. Over forty years ago, someone told my dad he looked like that actor, and Dad took that as a lifelong oath he must honor every single year.

Both of my parents have worn these costumes so much that it's how I picture them when we're not together—my dad with his cardboard ghost-busting backpack, and my mom in a poodle skirt with her hair in a curled ponytail that swishes from side to side as she flits through our art shop.

"We're so thrilled to have you learning from the great and powerful Darcy," Dad says, kissing me on the cheek as he addresses tonight's painters. Shifting his focus to the corner of the shop, he takes out his ghost gun and makes a show of pretending to attack an invisible intruder, adding in his own *pew-pew-pew* noises to go along with it.

My mom inspects my lips. "Where's the pink?" she whispers, voice full of concern.

"I ran out of lipstick."

The truth is, Grace gave me a red lip stain she didn't want, and she insisted I wear it tonight.

"I'll go out and get you some tomorrow morning," Mom says.

In our painting, the witch's lips are nothing more than a needle-fine prick with the smallest brush we provide. Changing my own lip color from pink to red is not going to rattle our customers' foundation of belief. Deep down, they have to already know I'm not a real witch. "Witch" is a title people give themselves when they want to read tarot, like Piper Blake's family, or when they need a good excuse to keep their spooky decorations up year-round.

I used to believe when I was a kid. Just like I believed in Santa Claus. The Easter Bunny. The tooth fairy. One by one, my parents revealed the truth about those other things. They haven't said anything about witches being fake, but they don't need to. They are real because collectively we commit to the idea that they could be. It's way too vital to Fableview to do otherwise.

But every change I make, no matter how small, rocks my parents to their cores. They won't even let me mend this old cape, afraid that patches of new fabric will detract from the garment's history. It's the cape my grandmother wore, and then my mother, and now me. As is the case with so many things around here.

"Now that our base is complete, it's time to turn our background into a real sky." I demonstrate the next steps as my parents walk down the rows of painters, offering gentle redirections. While we're supposed to encourage everyone's individual creativity, my parents don't like to see anyone walk out of here with a finished product that's strayed too far from our intended vision. We're so early in the process that it's hard to believe they have any instruction to give at all. Somehow, my mom and dad always find a way.

"I haven't seen Anya in about six minutes," Grace tells me, managing something close to a whisper now that my parents are downstairs with us.

"Are you running a stopwatch?" I ask.

"You know I have a very strong internal clock."

"Grace, this lovely woman could use your help perfecting her clouds," my mom announces. *She* could be the one to help, but what she really wants is for Grace to stop talking to me.

Grace hurries over to assist the painter while my mom swaps spots with her up front, plucking the paintbrush right out of my hands. "I'm sure Darcy already told you, but Halloween night in Fableview is always unbelievable," Mom says, streaking shades of green across my canvas. "The sky looks almost like the northern lights."

This kind of intrusion, my mom taking over my job for me, is not unfamiliar. Maybe because my parents had me so much later in life—they were forty-three when I was born, putting them both at sixty now—it doesn't bother me to have them hover over my every action. It's the way they've always been, praising me as their long-awaited miracle. Their precious baby girl they wanted more than anything in the world. It's not a responsibility I can escape. Accepting it makes life easier for everyone. They will always be too present, too involved. That doesn't mean I don't want a break every once in a while. Which is what college out of state could be.

If I can just find a good time to talk to them about it . . .

Almost all the kids in Fableview stick around after high school. Those who don't already work around here get jobs as soon as they can. Some go to the community college a few towns over to get their associate's degrees in something useful, but it's usually just to fill in whatever gaps are due to spring up in Fableview, like a new preschool teacher at the daycare or a technician at the vet. It's rare for anyone to actually leave for a four-year college. That's reserved for the teens who *really* know what they want. The future doctors and teachers, the scholarship athletes. Kids who have already made very firm decisions about what they want their lives to be.

I am not any of those things. I have good grades. I participate in a handful of extracurriculars. But my grades aren't super impressive, and I didn't pick my activities to be building blocks for padding out my college applications. They are just me exploring my interests, trying to figure out what compels me. I don't feel like I've made a firm decision about anything. Which is part of why I want the chance to see what life is like outside of Fableview. To maybe get the chance to learn something new about myself in the process.

As if realizing her overstep, my mom hands the brush back to me, blushing. "I'll let my Darcy show you," she says. "You couldn't be in better hands."

"Not only is the sky streaked with iridescent greens, but countless stars blanket the night here, making everything from the Big Dipper to the Scorpion visible to the trained eye," I say. "When I look up, I understand how big the world is. And it makes me eager to discover as much as I can."

This is my way of dropping a hint. It's all I've been brave enough to do, fearing the resistance I already know I will get. I expect to see my mom's face creased with concern, catching the hidden meaning in my speech. Instead she's smiling, pleased. She doesn't hear the truth in my words, even though she knows that almost every night, I lay in the hammock on the balcony attached to my bedroom, and I look up at the sky. When I see the stars above me, I wonder about everything beyond our strange little town. What do other people see at night? What would I see, living somewhere else?

"Lucky for us, our Darcy girl is here in Fableview," my dad says. "She'll be taking over our shop for us when we retire next year."

Grace lets out a gasp, as surprised by this reveal as I am. The painters clap like this is the best news they've heard all night. My mom squeezes my shoulder.

"What?" I'm careful to keep my voice measured, even as my mind spins.

My dad encourages a smile by painting an exaggerated one on his own face—always mindful of our customers. It's of utmost importance to my parents that we pull out all the stops every single night of October. This month is when we make over half of our money for the entire year. Not just our shop, but the entire town of Fableview.

"That's right," Dad says, voice spilling over with pride. "Our precious Darcy will be taking control of our beloved Halloween empire. Who could do it better than her?"

"No one!" Mom answers for him.

My mouth goes dry. All the words I want to say fight for purchase—the anger, the hurt, and the disappointment colliding. What do they mean I will take over *next year*? That's too soon. I haven't lived enough. I don't know who I am yet.

The front doorbell chimes, distracting all of us.

Anya Doyle stands in our shop like a cat that's stumbled into a dog convention, as skittish as she is oddly self-possessed, the unflinching intensity of her gaze never breaking, even as she reaches one arm protectively for her elbow.

I feel this overwhelming swell of gratitude for the interruption. Her presence has accomplished in two seconds what would've taken me minutes, if not hours, to do. By standing here, looking so out of place, she's stopped my parents from escalating this situation. If she hadn't arrived, they might've dug out a business contract for me to sign on the spot.

"I was wondering if . . ." she starts quietly. I make the mistake of stepping forward to hear her better, and she jerks back. "I should go." She hurries out the same way she hurried in, fast and erratic.

"I'll be right back," I tell my parents, following Anya out the door.

# 4

# ANYA

"What are you doing here?"

The question takes me by such surprise that I trip over the tiny barrier lining the flower beds, killing more asters with my clumsiness than I did with my powers.

It's Darcy's voice. She's always the first to raise her hand in class, responding even when she doesn't know an answer, just to keep the teacher from suffering up there without a participant. That's how kind she is. In the ten months since I moved to Fableview, she has never once sounded harsh or judgmental. Until right now.

With me.

I turn my head, and she's looming over me in her tiny pointed hat and cape. Is this what she thinks we wear? Anyone who knows a real witch would know that we prefer a hat with broader sun protection. And that cape would be impractical. The witches in my family need easy access to their hands. That's where most of us express our magic. A Doyle would be batting that off their arm every five seconds.

"I . . . forgot the French homework," I say.

French class is the only context through which Darcy knows me. It's also all that comes to mind with those sharp green eyes focused on mine. Maybe she remembers that time I forgot how to speak when she told me she liked my name, and I forgot again when she asked me the next day how I was liking the town. Or she has nightmares about that day Madame Poncik forced me to stand up and read two full pages of *Le Petit Prince* aloud.

Darcy's frustration turns into something worse. She's curious now, confused, her eyebrows scrunching into the bridge of her nose.

"Do you . . . do you know it? The homework?" I stumble out.

"Je fais. Et toi aussi." *I do. And so do you.*

"Non. J'oublié," I say, finding it easier to continue this conversation in French. Probably because I am making all this up and it helps to have to take an extra second to translate my thoughts.

"Vous êtes le meilleur élève de notre classe," she says back. *You're the best student in our class.*

My mind goes static, like I'm listening to someone speak a foreign language. Darcy *is* speaking a foreign language. But it's the focus of her attention that stops the processing center in my brain from functioning. There's a lag, not for translation but for comprehension of the impossibility of this situation.

Beautiful, confident Darcy Keller, with her shiny blond hair and her pouty red lips, has just told me I am the best student in our class. And while she is right—I have a 107 percent average at the moment, and Madame Poncik has already told me more than once to stop doing unnecessary extra credit—it's not something I discuss with others. If anything, I'm embarrassed by my aggressive commitment to learning French. What else am I going to do in the only class that Darcy and I share? Stare at her so hard that she gets a sunburn from the force of my admiration?

When I fail to be initiated into my family's coven, maybe I can move to France. It might be the most viable option I have. All the places I've already lived are places where my family also lives. In France no one would know me. No one would care about the legacy of my name. They wouldn't mourn the loss of my ability to mend something.

I'd be normal.

But I'd also be alone. And that's the most terrifying prospect of all.

"You know, you can find the homework on the portal," Darcy reminds me.

"Of course," I say, remembering in earnest. All our homework assignments get uploaded to Fableview High's online portal. Which would have occurred to me if Darcy hadn't surprised me out here, demanding answers.

She reaches out a hand to help me stand. There's still ash from my disintegrated flower there, and I feel the rough texture of what I've killed between the softness of our linked palms.

Once I'm upright, Darcy stands a good three inches shorter than me, all grit and determination. She puts her hands on her hips, waiting for further explanation.

"I'll let you get back to work," I say, walking away. "Sorry for interrupting your class."

*"Wait."* Her heeled boots let out loud clacks, increasing in urgency with every step.

We stop in front of the metaphysical shop a few buildings down from Pam's Paints. There is a gigantic chunk of rose quartz in the window, framed by a sign that says WITCHES OF FABLEVIEW in bright pink neon. The glow washes Darcy's face in monochrome, turning her into a rose-colored vision.

"I'm actually taking a little breather from my parents right now," she tells me.

*Same*, I think, even though my parents are over two thousand miles away, high-fiving each other because they believe my best friend is the girl standing in front of me in a witch's costume—a descendant of a legacy protector family, ready to take on the role of protecting *me* for the rest of our lives.

"What have they done now?" I ask.

Darcy surprises me with a laugh. "Have you met my parents?"

"No. But parents are always doing something. Historically."

She laughs again. "You walked into them announcing my role as the next owner of Pam's Paints. Which would've been fine, if it weren't for the fact that no one discussed it with me beforehand. At least not in a *next year you're going to own this place* way. It's sort of implied that everyone stays here after high school. Unless you show some great, impressive talent that requires you to go to a four-year college. I'm not impressive at anything other than working at Pam's Paints."

Darcy is the president of Fableview High's art club. She sings in the school choir, where she regularly performs solos. Her hair is always perfectly brushed and curled. She smells like strawberries dipped in vanilla. She has always given me the impression that she bends to no one's will. To me there is not a single other person our age in Fableview who seems more in charge of their own life than Darcy Keller.

And for what it's worth, there is no one more impressive either.

"Do you not want to own the art shop?" I ask.

She makes a scoffing sound, insulted by the question in a way that would require me to have a lot more context about the situation than I do. She seems to realize this herself, because she unfolds her arms, leaning herself against the Witches of Fableview shop window.

"The thing is, my parents don't want anything to change. *Ever*," she says. "They're so obsessed with tradition that they don't realize how hard it is to perfectly re-create every detail of our lives each fall. Not that I can't do it. I can."

"I believe you," I say.

Her look is laced with mistrust, as if she can't quite figure out what I have to gain by flattering her. "It's just a lot of work. They don't want me to wear a different costume or hang a new kind of twinkle light in front of our building. Passing this shop over to me is a symbolic gesture. They just want to know their only child has security over the paperwork. And I guess I would've liked a little say in the matter."

Her life is so different from mine, but her problems still feel like my own. I've never had a job, for one. Learning how to be a witch *is* my job. Some of the members of our coven work, but most live on the trust funds every witch gains access to upon initiation on their eighteenth birthday. Keeping everyone in our coven connected, making sure the communities where we live continue to thrive—that's the real work of a Doyle. It's a tradition everyone in the family is expected to keep up. Not only am I the first witch in centuries to potentially fail my initiation, but I seem to be the first to not really enjoy being a witch at all.

"They just want to make sure our family's role as the planners of Fableview's Halloween festivities doesn't get snatched up by the Holtzenbergs," Darcy adds.

The last name is familiar, but I can't place it, so I say, "That sounds like a lot of pressure."

"I like pressure." The challenge in her voice intensifies. "That's not the problem."

"I've heard Halloween is a big deal around here," I try, no longer sure where to go with this conversation. Even my kindest words seem to offend her. "Everyone wears costumes every single day?"

"Oh yeah. You haven't seen anything yet."

"Surely you could wear a different costume, though? There are thirty-one days in the month. You need to wash that cloak sometime."

Darcy laughs again. Quick. Full.

I'm not funny.

Am I?

"So take this paint night, for example," she says. "We've taught the same artwork for longer than I've been alive. A witch on a broomstick, flying over the forest. Grace and I wanted to add a tiny dog to the painting. Grace came up with a good backstory for it too. We make all this up anyway, so I'm not sure why my parents care so much. It's not like witches are real. Leaning into all this stuff is a business decision that keeps Fableview afloat. Anyway, the actual change we made to the painting amounts to, like, five tiny brushstrokes. Still, my parents freaked out about us teaching that version to the tourists. They wouldn't let us do it."

*It's not like witches are real.*

For someone who is supposedly from a protector family, she hasn't said this with any kind of hidden wink. Maybe that's her version of protection? Could she really believe that in a town like Fableview? Aunt Cal and I aren't the only witches who live here. We're standing in front of a store called Witches of Fableview, after all. But, to my knowledge, we *are* the only coven that seeks out protectors. Every coven has different rules, and in the Doyle family, having a protector is a practice that stretches back to our earliest times in Ireland.

There's a story attached to it—there's always a story—about a Doyle witch from hundreds of years ago who was moments from being killed for her gift, until she came up with a solution that appealed to everyone. She realized that the mortals hated her for having something they would never have. Making them a part of her magic by asking them to look out for her, to keep her safe, is what stopped them from killing her. She used her magic to keep the town's crops healthy, bringing good fortune and prosperity to the area. And in exchange, she got to stay alive. It's always sounded like more of a desperate trade-off than an actual act of kindness from the mortals.

Whether or not this actually happened anyway is impossible to say. My family's stories feel more like folklore than truth from where I'm sitting, passed down and reshaped through generations to fit whatever lesson needs to be taught. What's not lost on me is that my ancestor's powers sound a lot like my own. I might be the second coming of the witch who created our coven's entire structure, and I'm the first one in the family line who doesn't seem capable of following the rules she set forth.

I already tried once to ask a mortal to be my protector. Her name was Julia, and I thought she was my best friend. But I was wrong. Very, very wrong. So it's a little hard to buy into the feel-good family narrative about our beautiful, enduring connection to mortals.

Darcy eyes me expectantly. If this conversation is a test, every question I ask must be precise.

"What kind of dog?" I choose.

"It's just a cute little basset hound," she says.

"Should've done a wolfhound," I respond without thinking, forgetting to accept her assertion that witches aren't real.

This knocks Darcy out of whatever internal spiral she's been in, reminding her that her audience for this is me, a stranger. An outsider.

"Don't tell me you believe in witches," she says. She reaches behind my ear, and my breath hitches at the nearness of her. She smells as sweet as always. Her hand is so soft.

I could die. I really could.

She procures a coin. It's pressed into an oval shape and imprinted with a picture of a jack-o'-lantern.

"Someone else would tell you that's magic," she whispers. "But *I* will tell you the truth. Anyone who says they have real powers around here has just watched some YouTube tutorials on magic tricks."

"I don't know," I say. "That seemed pretty real to me. There's no way you're walking around carrying specialty coins in your pockets."

"Of course I am. We keep them in this cape to use on little kids who come into the shop." She looks me up and down, lingering on my face for so long that my hands start sweating. "Or high school French students."

It's hard to meet her eye. She's just *so* confident, even now when she's completely wrong.

"It's fun to pretend, though," she continues. "That's what makes Halloween the best holiday of them all. It's all about the art of make-believe. And I love to imagine things. I just don't mistake my imagination for reality. So if you see something here you can't explain . . ."

"Someone learned how to do it on YouTube," I finish.

"Exactly." She smiles, pleased. "Or it's a natural phenomenon. I've definitely seen a lot of what Mother Nature can do while living here."

"She's powerful," I say.

"She is. So, tell me why you're here."

She's been very vulnerable, honest despite her obvious defenses, that maybe I *should* do the same in return. Maybe that's the only way out of all this.

"The truth is . . ." I start, clearing my throat before I say the rest.

Darcy's eyes widen. Green like spring. Green as hope.

"I'm a witch."

"Shut up," she says.

"I'm serious."

We stare at each other for what feels like a lifetime. What looks at first to be a true, deep understanding dawning on her face turns out to be . . .

Laughter.

"I never knew you were this funny," she says, grabbing my arm to steady herself.

"Neither did I."

She smiles expectantly, waiting for the truth that's supposed to follow my punch line.

Pulsing with a new wave of adrenaline, I say, "Actually, I'm here because I want to take your art class."

"You . . . what?"

"I came here to take your art class," I repeat. Beads of sweat break through on my forehead. "I always see signs for the shop around town. And since it's October, it feels like the right time to try it out. Is it too late to join?"

"Not at all," she says. "Follow me."

So I do.

I'm not ready to walk away anymore either. Darcy Keller is the perfect girl, and not because she's beautiful, funny, and smart. Darcy is perfect because she doesn't believe in magic. My powers don't matter to her. Instead of asking her about the dinner or about being my protector, I can use her as a template.

Darcy Keller can show me how a mortal makes a living.

And maybe, if I'm lucky, I can pull her out of another bad mood in the process.

# 5

# DARCY

"I like the gnome," Anya says as she follows me into our shop.

The wall behind the register is covered in dozens of ceramics we've painted over the years. There is a collection of fairies my mom's been adding to since she was a teen. There are plates my dad has done with different landscapes, because he's really good at painting trees and he never misses an opportunity to show it off. There are seasonal pieces from my grandmother that we put out every Halloween—ceramic pumpkins, ghosts, and cats that are older than I am. All of it is better than the break time craft I did in thirty minutes during last spring's Paintapalooza.

"I made that," I tell her.

"I figured," she says, in such a casual but knowing way that my mind continues racing, undoing ten months of English silence and French conjugations, searching for gaps when we've somehow communicated without words. More than once tonight she's mentioned things about me that I'd never have expected her to notice.

Taking in the wall of ceramics, I try to look past all the obviously better creations and find my gnome worth noting. I painted little hearts on his stocking cap. Did his sweater in a checkered pattern. He's very sweet, but he's nothing special. How could she possibly know he was mine?

There's not a lot I understand about this moment, but there's one thing I know for sure—Anya Doyle did not come here to learn the French homework. She didn't come here to take my art class either. But she *does* provide the perfect distraction from what my parents have done.

"We have a late arrival," I tell my parents. "My friend from school, Anya."

*"Friend?"* Grace makes no effort to hide her skepticism.

"Yeah, you know Anya," I say, giving Grace a little *just go with it* glare.

Grace plays along to the extent she can, which is to say the right things with the look of a startled deer watching headlights inch closer, incapable of moving out of the line of fire. "Hey, girl! Glad to have you."

"Hi," Anya says back flatly.

It's not supposed to be funny, but it makes me laugh all the same. She's just so herself, even when it makes other people uncomfortable. I can't help but find it endearing.

"We don't allow late arrivals," my dad reminds me, once again using the same smile he tried to have me paint onto my own face earlier.

I place Anya in front of a blank canvas at the end of the middle row of painters. "Surely we can make an exception for the newest member of Fableview's Fall Planning Committee. She came here tonight to tell me she wanted to join."

My parents swap their skepticism for open enthusiasm.

"How fantastic!" Mom says. "We can always use extra help-ing hands around town! Welcome, Anya!"

"I'll explain in a bit," I whisper into Anya's ear. This close to her, I smell herbs I associate with Witches of Fableview, the metaphysical shop the Blake family owns down the street. I don't know the herbs' names, but they are scents that make me think of magic. If it were real, it would smell like this—an earthy, con-suming potion of petals and oils.

Returning to my canvas, I slide back into the role of Darcy the art teacher, no comment made about my parents' earlier announcement. There's nothing more to say on the matter. At least, not now. I can't involve the tourists in my personal drama. Not during peak season.

Anya catches up fast, painting her background and speck-ling it with stars. When we move on to adding in the trees, she watches me with unwavering focus. It's . . . intense to be the subject of her attention. She doesn't make any faces to urge me forward. No friendly smiles when I attempt my little jokes. No thoughtful nods of appreciation when I demonstrate how to stip-ple the brush for greenery.

My toes grip my shoes, fighting to keep blood from rushing to my cheeks. This is just how she is. Even when Madame Pon-cik pairs us up to conjugate verbs together, she is like this. It's not personal.

By the time we're adding the actual witch to the painting, I've almost adjusted to the way it feels to have her watch me. I like the challenge of it, the way it makes me consider my every movement in a way I normally wouldn't.

Grace has grabbed my arm no less than four times—

a reminder that we will be having a *conversation* about this as soon as we're done with our shift. At present, all is calm.

Until Anya raises her hand.

"What about the dog?" she asks.

The painters crane their necks, peering at her in the back. I think of the time Madame Poncik forced her to stand up and read *Le Petit Prince* out loud. Her shoulders had rounded forward as her eyes burned holes into the pages, yet she'd read with flawless accented French, not only technically correct but filled with emotion too.

She does not like this kind of attention. Yet she's offered herself up.

For me.

"The basset hound," she adds, like maybe I haven't understood her. "I just, I notice that you're dressed exactly like the witch in the painting." Everyone has stilled their paintbrushes. Even the tourists seem to sense how rare this moment is. "So are we going to add the dog that looks like her?" She points to Grace, who does a bashful *who me?* bat of her hand, embracing the attention.

"That's not part of the paint—" my mom starts.

"We can," I interrupt. If someone as normally reserved as Anya Doyle can take a leap of faith, I can take one right back. "Grace, will you grab the basset hound version from the back?"

Grace—torn between disobeying my parents and getting to share the basset hound story she created—takes a step forward, then immediately steps back.

"Never mind," I say. My mom exhales an audible sigh of relief. "I'll get it." I head for our supply closet, and my mom and dad follow, the three of us closing ourselves inside without more than a foot to spare.

"You can't teach that," my mom whispers, putting her hand in front of the rack of witch paintings, blocking me from reaching for it.

"The artists have already put in a background and scenery," my dad adds, like that's the real reason.

"Anya asked for it," I say.

"She seems lovely, but we're not bringing out a brand-new painting for someone who couldn't even get the start time right."

"Please," I beg.

"No," Dad says firmly.

For some reason, tears threaten to surface. It's not about this painting, I know. But also, it kind of is. They're making such a big deal about this very small thing when surely it's a bigger deal to tell me that I'm going to run this whole art shop *next year*. If they can't handle this change to the painting, they'll never accept the news that I want to go to college out of state.

It bothers me that they've never once asked me if I want something different. They just assume I'll stay here after high school, because it's what they did when they were my age, and they expect me to be their spitting image in every way.

The shop has always been called Pam's Paints. My grandma named it for my mom when she opened it, thrusting this legacy upon my mom as a baby. Grandma and Grandpa used up almost all the money they had to make this dream of having an art shop happen. They had to move into the condo above this building because it was all they could afford at the time, and it made it easy to spend every waking minute here, thinking up ways to keep not just the shop but our entire town afloat. They're the ones who started the Fableview Fall Planning Committee.

Within a few years, they'd turned our once floundering town into a genuine Halloween empire.

My dad grew up here too, taking art classes from my grandma and, eventually, from my mom. That's how they fell in love. Right here in this shop.

Neither of them knows a world outside of Fableview—outside of Pam's Paints, even. And they don't want to. Which is why they can't imagine one for me either.

I am their precious baby girl. Their greatest hope. The child they waited so long to have, and the only person they'll ever trust with our family's work.

This is who I was born to be.

"Okay," I say to them, forcing myself to smile.

They give me a joint hug. "We love you," they say in unison.

"I know," I tell them. "I love you too."

I return to my spot in front of the painters. With my biggest, brightest smile, I apologize for the misunderstanding about the dog, and I continue teaching the class as planned.

Eventually, my parents retreat upstairs.

When we finish the painting, I hope Anya will just leave. Everything I said to her outside seems mortifying now. Why did I ramble about not wanting to own the art shop next year?

She *doesn't* leave. In fact, she waits out every single enthusiastic tourist, even the ones who stick around to take pictures with me beside their paintings. She stays in her seat, staring at her completed canvas until it's only me, her, and Grace left in the shop.

Grace is, of course, allergic to normalizing this. With every paintbrush she rinses off, she makes a show of smacking it as loud as she can against the edge of the sink. If we were in a restaurant,

Grace would be turning over every chair around Anya to make a point. She'd be mopping the floor and asking Anya to pick up her feet so she could get under them.

"Is everything okay?" I finally ask Anya, unable to withstand another moment of this silent showdown.

Her natural expression is already downturned, but she's frowning even harder than usual, her face a perfect portrait of disappointment. How could she possibly care enough to think I've let her down by not painting the basset hound?

And why do *I* care?

"The planning committee," she says.

Embarrassment steals all my cool. I projected an entire tortured inner monologue onto her reason for hanging around when really she's just waiting for me to explain myself.

"Oh, I'm sorry," I say. Heat burns my face. "My parents hate late arrivals, but they love getting new committee members. It was the only way they'd let you join the class."

"I see." She stands up, her posture so rigid, she could balance a stack of books on her head.

"But if you want to join, we'd really appreciate it," I add before she can flee. "We have weekly meetings at city hall. The next one is tomorrow after school. There's no pressure to come. But it's at five, if you can make it."

Anya says nothing. She doesn't even turn around to acknowledge my words.

"What the *hell* was that?" Grace asks the second the bell above the door is done chiming.

"I wish I knew," I tell her, watching Anya stalk down Fableview Boulevard and following her movements until she's no longer visible.

25 Days Until Halloween

# 6

## ANYA

I don't take other people's feelings into consideration. That's what my so-called best friend Julia once told me. It was the kind of gut punch cruelty that part of me knew she said just to hurt my feelings. But another part of me felt the hard kernel of truth within it, the kind that gets caught in your mind the way popcorn gets stuck in teeth. Instead of finding some way to remove it, I've grown around it, absorbing this belief as a part of my personality. I don't think about other people enough. I am not sensitive to what they need from me. If anyone is ever going to like me, I have to change this about myself.

So if I hope for Darcy Keller to enjoy my presence enough to let me learn the ways of being mortal through being around her, I need to figure out what she wants from me. Which is to attend this committee meeting.

Slipping into the back row of the only conference room at Fableview's city hall, I scan the crowd. There are a few people dressed up even for this—an old man with a long beard, wearing a wizard robe. Or maybe he *is* a wizard. Tough to say in a town like this. Not that Darcy would think twice about it. She'd assume he was performing.

There are two middle-aged women dressed as matching bumblebees. Another woman done up as a medieval wench.

For a moment, I panic, wondering if the sensitive thing to do would've been to dress up too. But I don't own anything other than black clothes. I could've gotten some cat ears, I guess. Darcy would have probably seen that as an insulting lack of effort.

When she steps up to the podium, I'm relieved to see she's in the same outfit she had on at school—a short blue dress with daisies on it. She has two small clips on either side of her head, leaving her bangs to frame her face while pulling the longer pieces out of the way so her blond ringlets can do their waterfall cascade thing down her back.

She takes the time to look at each member of the committee and smile. When she gets to me, I can't help but look away, sure that my crush is tattooed on my face. I stare down at my phone, pretending my lock screen shows me something far more interesting than Darcy Keller.

"I know you were expecting my parents, but they're busy with preparations for this weekend, so they've asked me to run today's meeting. Please forgive me if I get anything wrong," she says.

She looks happy up there. But she's always been good in front of a crowd. It would be rarer to see her look upset. Is this the first task of her future role? A warm-up commitment from her parents to prepare her for taking over?

"Before we get started, we have a new committee member in

the audience. I know she won't want too much fanfare, so let's just say a very quick welcome to Anya." Darcy gestures to me, and everyone begins applauding.

This committee is made up of people of all ages. There are a handful of our classmates, including Grace Manalo, who gives me the same glare she gave me at the art shop. She even puts two fingers to her eyes and then points them at mine, mouthing, *I'm watching you*. That doesn't bother me much. It's gotten easy to tolerate people disliking me.

But being welcoming? I don't know what to do with that. I try my best to fix my face into something less scowl-like for the applauding crowd.

"Okay. That's enough," Darcy says. "I don't want to overwhelm her. Thank you for being here, Anya."

My throat's too dry to respond. My hand won't lift to wave either. She has somehow managed to find the exact amount of attention I can handle without shriveling into dust, and still, I can't move.

"All right. On to the first order of business," she continues. "The costume parade barriers."

This gets varied reactions from the committee. Some whoops and, to my surprise, even a groan.

"I know, I know," Darcy says. "My parents and I just want to be extra sure that *no one* needs new barriers for the sidewalks. We don't want to have a repeat of what happened last year."

It's the wizard gentleman who is displeased. He lets out another sound—a throaty scoff this time—as he says, "I didn't realize my ropes were broken until that morning."

Darcy gives him a smile so inviting in return that it's almost sinister how good she is at letting his obvious rudeness bounce right off her. "Exactly. Which is why we're asking that everyone go home and check their supplies tonight."

He scoffs again, mumbling, "Ridiculous," and tossing his hands up.

I'm still stuck on twenty seconds ago when I didn't acknowledge Darcy's welcoming. My hand shoots up before my mind can third-guess the action.

"Oh," Darcy says, eyebrows lifted in what is hopefully delighted shock. "Anya, yes."

"I was wondering . . . what the costume parade is, exactly," I say.

"Sorry for not explaining."

I sink into my seat, fighting off the blush that wants to rise to my cheeks. "I'm sure it's exactly what it sounds like. I just . . . wanted to know more."

She nods in encouragement. "Of course. I'm happy to do that. We shut down Fableview Boulevard and some of the surrounding side streets, and we hold a parade. Little kids walk down the street in costumes. Business owners hand out candy as the kids pass. People bring their families in from out of town to participate. It's very sweet."

"Do the businesses offer anything other than candy for the attendees?" I ask.

The people who clapped for my presence have now turned their torsos a full 180 degrees to see me. I'm not inexperienced in the art of derision. Most people find me off-putting. But it's rare even for me to have gained and lost the favor of an entire room in a matter of only a few minutes. Grace's taunting seems tame in comparison to the open annoyance now being hurled my way.

"You're all already dressed in costumes, right?" I continue, finding myself wanting their approval. Or to prove my role here. Darcy has gone out of her way to make me feel welcome. I can't be the one everyone hates. Not already.

"You know, we *could* have personalized shop tie-ins," Darcy says. "Each of us could offer something unique! Discounts for people who return in our offseason."

"Maybe even your own kind of parade inside the shops," I suggest. "Like, everyone has to stop inside, and somehow it could build so each shop could give you a reason to go to the next one for something?"

We volley back and forth a little longer. It's surprisingly easy to talk to Darcy, even in front of a crowd. She seems eager to hear me out. Excited by what I'm saying. What we come up with sounds fun, even to me, a person who has never once voluntarily attended a *parade*.

With his most theatrical, grunting noise of displeasure yet, the same older wizard from earlier interrupts us to ask, "Why would we need to change what we already know works perfectly?"

He doesn't even sound judgmental. He's calm, rational. Why would this town branch out when they've had success doing things the way they always have?

I think of my family's coven. How we've functioned the same way for generations, asking our witches to bring mortal friends to our initiations to pledge loyalty to our coven, with no consideration of whether that's even necessary anymore.

Our ancestor was almost killed for her magic hundreds of years ago. Times have changed. Not to mention the fact that we get initiated on our eighteenth birthday, and we have to pick people who will protect our coven for the rest of our *lives*. Every town I've ever lived in, the adults make mention of how the things I do as a teen may not reflect who I will one day become. They say it about my clothes, telling me that maybe one day, I'll like wearing something other than black. They say it about the music I listen to, promising me I won't want to play only sad stuff. It will get depressing once I'm an adult, and I'll want a break from that feeling. They say it about my personality, telling me I'll grow out of being sullen.

To them, everything about me is a supposed phase. And that's always been annoying, because I *know* myself. I know what I like and what I want, and it doesn't make me any better or worse than them just because I haven't been alive as long as they have. It's ironic that choosing a protector is the only thing they trust me to make a good decision about, and it's this huge, life-altering choice. I'm supposedly this hormonal, ever-changing creature of the night as a teenager, but also, I need to pick a friend who can look out for me until my dying breath?

"What if something else works better?" I challenge, forgetting for a second that this wizard is a stranger, not a member of my family's coven. I should keep my mouth shut. But I can't help but wonder—why can't we want things to be better than they are? Why can't we try something different?

"I don't think any of us are in the mood to experiment," the wizard tells me.

Darcy takes a quick breath to regroup. She tosses back her

long blond hair as she moves to the next item on her agenda. She's so good at letting things roll off her back.

I don't think a single thing has ever rolled off mine.

The rest of the meeting, I remain quiet. I'm just an outsider, after all. Always an outsider. The most considerate thing I can do in this situation is to shut up.

When Darcy dismisses us, I attempt to slink out, hurrying down the hallway to beat the rush. I make it all the way through the exit and onto the street when Darcy calls my name.

One word, and my arms tingle, goose bumps prickling across my flesh.

She jogs to meet me as several other committee members file past us. She waves goodbyes, making promises to talk to them soon about other matters brought up during the meeting. But she doesn't move. She has one foot planted forward, almost stepping between my legs.

"Thanks for coming today," she says once the rest of the committee is gone.

"Of course," I tell her. There are a dozen conversation starters I wish I had, but none come to mind, so I leave it at that, hoping my sincerity has broken through the constant rain cloud that is my general disposition.

She places a hand on my shoulder. My goose bumps get electrified by the contact, pinpricks of excitement threatening to make me do something reckless, like smile. "We can still change things, you know."

"I think the wizard guy would place a curse on us if we do," I say.

She laughs. "He might. Which is why we won't tell anyone

we're doing it." The way she's grinning is a death blow to my rain cloud.

How could I do anything but smile in return?

She hands me a piece of paper with several dates and activities listed. "This is the full schedule for the month of October," she says.

There are so many events on it that I'm exhausted just reading it—a costume parade, a pumpkin patch party, an apple bobbing contest, a haunted carnival. Something called the Fall Ball happening the night before Halloween, described as a townwide dance that requires formalwear.

"I know," Darcy says, reading along with me. "It's a lot. But that means we have plenty of chances to try stuff out. No one here will ever let us do anything new if we ask. We have to show them that it can work first. If you're still in, that is."

There's a flicker of optimism in her eyes, the tiniest bit of trust that I can't believe I've earned. If I really tried, I could easily come up with a convincing reason to turn her down.

But I don't want to try. I want to be the kind of person Darcy Keller believes in.

"I'm in," I say.

# 20 Days Until Halloween

# 7

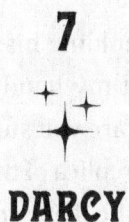

# DARCY

My fairy wings keep clanking against our wall of ceramics. More than once I've had to make a hero save, stopping one of our family masterpieces from crashing to the floor. This isn't my first time wearing this costume. I've never had a problem navigating our front desk space in it before. Somehow, my sense of place has shifted, like everything in my world has been moved a fraction of an inch, and I no longer know how to get around like I used to.

I keep turning to look out the window directly to my left, watching for Anya. She told me she was going to come today. Why would she bother to say that at the planning meeting if she didn't mean it? Even though I saw her every day in French class this week, I couldn't bring myself to turn around and ask her. We don't exist that way to each other in school.

She seems to agree, because she hasn't said anything either.

Outside of school, though, she's stuck her neck out for me *twice*—once at the shop, and again at the planning meeting. There's no way she'd ghost me now.

Right?

Our front door chimes, and I get a crick in my neck from glancing up so fast. It's not Anya. It is the least Anya person to ever exist.

Kyle Holtzenberg.

*"Daaaaaarce,"* he says, holding his hand up for me to high-five. When I reluctantly lift my hand to match it, he pulls his own back. "Too slow! What are you supposed to be? A bird?"

My costume is an exact replica of the spring fairy figurine directly behind me, down to the daisy crown on my head and the butterfly perched on my shoulder. Even without that context, it's *so* obvious that I am a fairy. There is nothing birdlike about what I'm wearing, except for the presence of wings. But they are whimsical, glittery wings. Fairy wings.

"I'm working right now," I say.

Kyle grips the back of his neck. He's gotten a fresh haircut, sharp auburn edges that contrast the hundreds of round freckles smattered across his face. "Aw, c'mon. It's like that now?"

"It's like that," I confirm.

"Then I take it you're not trying to go with me to the Fall Ball?"

"You've taken it correctly."

"Not even if I promise to get a better-fitting tux this year? My mom said she'll take me to the mall. My arms have bulked up too much from all the lifting I've been doing." He kisses one of his biceps, flexing it so I can see the muscle definition.

Kyle Holtzenberg and I first dated in sixth grade, when Grace dared us to kiss behind the middle school dumpsters. That exchange has bonded us together in ways that can never be undone, because it's Fableview, and everything that happens here becomes some kind of unbreakable tradition. As a result, Kyle has been the guy I sort of talk to sometimes. I wouldn't even call it dating. He's just always *around*, and so am I.

Occasionally, we're around together.

Last year, gazing up at the sky from my hammock as I so often do, I had my first of many panics about my future. I thought that maybe I'd been wrong to dump Kyle in sixth grade. Maybe Kyle and I really *were* endgame. It made sense on paper, and, well, it's Fableview. My parents found each other here, and everything else about my life had so far aligned with theirs.

So I let Kyle take me to the Fall Ball. He got me a corsage. I got him a boutonniere. His tie matched my dress. It was all shaping up to be a decent idea on my part. There was no chemistry between us, but he could be funny when he wanted, and I hoped I could grow into our relationship the same way I'd grown into bad haircuts.

*His* parents were ecstatic, and I pretended not to notice all their little comments about the Holtzenbergs finally getting in on my family's Halloween empire.

All night, Kyle would not stop trying to lift me up over his head. The entire evening, every song, it was his singular focus—to lift me over his head. We tried it at least ten times. It was embarrassing from the very first failed attempt, but Kyle would not relent. He couldn't let it go, and at a certain point, I became invested in helping him figure it out.

Finally, on the last song of the night, he succeeded.

As he held me up, I admit, the moment was cool. But it was a bittersweet kind of cool. With all our friends gathered around us, sweaty and cheering, gazing up at me as Kyle death-gripped my rib cage, I saw my entire future. Marrying Kyle. Him lifting me up the same way at our wedding. Us owning Pam's Paints together. Taking over the condo from my parents. Running the annual Fableview fall extravaganza.

And it all seemed ... fine?

It wasn't bad. It's nice when things are planned in advance. I appreciate a template, and my parents have given me an excellent one. But I *love* a challenge. I love when my classes get harder and I feel like I have to sit up straighter and really listen to my teachers to understand. I love when someone brings me a problem they think they can't solve, and we put our minds together to come up with a solution. I love when my friends have different opinions than mine, because it forces me to sharpen my own—to *really* understand why I believe something or, sometimes, why I shouldn't.

I didn't see any room for that in my imagined future with Kyle. I saw everything I already knew.

Which is why I went home and looked up colleges out of state for the very first time. It felt dangerous. Risky. Something I could only do with all the lights off and the covers pulled over my head.

But it also felt exciting. I loved looking at the different campuses, imagining myself there. Was I the type of person who'd want to go to school near the beach? Or did I want to live in the cornfields at one of those state schools in the middle of nowhere? Maybe I was meant for navigating college in the big city while learning the subway system. I wasn't sure which place would suit me best, which was what I liked the most.

Everything in Fableview is fixed. And my potential life outside of here is unpredictable.

I told myself that looking at colleges didn't have to mean anything. I was just browsing, the same way I do when I get an ad for a cute shirt on social media.

But the more time that passed, the harder it became to give up. I kept looking at colleges. Every night, I'd browse campuses before I fell asleep. By the time my junior year ended, I'd taken both the ACT and the SAT without my parents knowing.

It wasn't hard to do. I have my own bank account thanks to working at Pam's Paints, so I paid for both tests myself. And because it was our offseason at the shop, my parents didn't think too hard about me being gone for a few hours. I told them I was off studying.

In a way, I was. Studying for what a future could look like outside of our home. A lot of colleges don't require either test score anymore, but I figured if I did well, it certainly wouldn't hurt.

And I *did* do well. Better than I even expected. At that point, I thought, *Well, surely I can't waste these good scores. That would be a shame. Might as well see what they can do for me.*

So when college application windows opened up this past August, I found myself applying to one school. Only one.

Just to see.

I won't find out if I got in until next year. Plenty of time to decide what it means.

And it all started at last year's Fall Ball.

Ever since that night, it's been easy to see Kyle as a comedian of sorts, whose whole bit is pretending we're in love. He doesn't believe it, doesn't really mean it. He just hasn't experienced anything different. If I ever get out of here, he'll be able to find someone else who can appreciate all his biceps kisses and failed high fives.

"Have you ever considered that maybe you're too good for me?" I ask him, attempting the brave and possibly reckless move of pulling a reverse UNO on him, if only to stop myself from checking the window so often. "We both know I'm not the gym rat princess of passion you deserve."

"Damn," he says, genuinely rocked. "Nah, I hadn't really given that any thought." He looks up at the painted ceramics behind me and points to the fairy. "Is that the bird you're trying to be?"

"Yes."

He does a little fist pump for himself. *"Nice."* Then he does his favorite kind of smile, the one he thinks makes him look like a charming prince, which I wish he'd never told me, but unfortunately, he did.

*"Don't I look like a charming prince when I do this?"*

*"Do you mean Prince Charming?"*

*"No, I mean, like, any prince who's charming. I think I'm kind of my own prince. Don't you?"*

"Are you sure you don't want to go with me, Darce?" he asks, tilting his chin down in his princely way. "One-last-date-for-us-as-seniors kinda thing? I could lift you over my head so easily now. I know what I was missing last year. I wasn't engaging my core. Kind of embarrassing when I look back. Obviously I needed the support of my trunk."

"I don't want you to take this too personally, but I will never be with someone from Fableview," I tell him, saying it with so much intensity that he actually backs up a few steps. "There is not a single person in this town who could ever excite me enough to want to date them."

The front door chimes.

I stand so fast, my wings crash into the ceramics above. Three go sailing to the ground—*smash, smash, smash* in rapid succession.

Kyle turns to see who's gotten this reaction. When all he sees is Anya, he looks around, like surely someone else has entered with her.

Someone else *has* entered with her—a woman with similar brown eyes and the same downturned mouth. Quick memories slot into place. All the times I've seen this woman around town through the years. She's reserved, much like Anya, though much more eccentric, always in that patchwork quilt jacket and a large sun hat. This must be the aunt Anya lives with. The one Grace told me is equally as sinister as Anya.

I bend down to pick up the ceramic pieces. I've broken a fairy from my mom's collection. A mug my dad painted before I was born. It wasn't anything fancy, but as a young kid, I used to stare at it, transfixed by the uniformity of the dots, each one exactly spaced from the one before it. And I've broken the gnome.

It's only some ceramics. But to my family, this is our whole entire world. It's hard not to see it as a warning—this is what happens when I'm reckless.

Who else could take over this shop but me? Who else could look down at these broken pieces and know they need to be reassembled?

No one.

No matter what happens with the college I applied to, I have to stay in Fableview.

Maybe the changes Anya and I are going to make around here can be for the future me. The owner of Pam's Paints me. At least then I can make sure that I'm around to fix anything that might break.

I can keep our town's magic alive.

# 8

# ANYA

Aunt Cal's presence is the equivalent of an ant on a sandwich, trudging along with unbroken determination. Everywhere I go, she follows, chasing my actions without speaking words.

She has the magical power of foresight. It's not as much of a benefit as one might hope, especially because of its unpredictable nature. She can see the future. She just can't always control *what* future she sees. Or when she sees it. Which is why she's decided to give up speaking, believing that the loss of one sense will heighten this other one. It's something one of her mentors had her try when she was still an apprentice, as I am. She's gotten very into using eggs as scribes, dropping them into water and watching the way the yolk splays, using that as an additional divination device to aid her visions.

It's *also* why she got that far-off look this afternoon when I told her I was heading out to the costume parade. She made a wait-for-me gesture with her hands, then proceeded to spend another hour doing random things around the house, making me arrive at Pam's Paints much later than I planned. If only I could just *say* this to Darcy, who's holding back tears over the ceramics she's just shattered. But Darcy doesn't believe in real witches in the first place, and Cal is listening to my every word, so all I can manage is a "Sorry I'm late. Here, let me help."

"I didn't even notice." Darcy blocks my hand from grabbing the broom tucked into a corner behind her. "And I've got it, thanks." Something jagged in her tone, as broken as the ceramics on the floor, tells me she *did* notice. And she cared.

My chest already aches seeing her this way—distraught over what's been broken. She keeps looking away as she wipes her tears.

I glance over my shoulder at Cal, who is holding up one of the shop's many witch figurines and examining it with an uncensored grimace. If Aunt Cal would speak, she'd surely say something along the lines of "Purple striped socks? *Please.*"

"My aunt wouldn't let me leave sooner," I whisper to Darcy. "She hates being early. She thinks it's embarrassing. I'm really sorry."

Darcy doesn't quite smile, but she's less despairing. "It's okay." She wipes another tear. "I made some cards I thought we could pass out. I just need to finish sweeping this up first. I'm sure I can glue everything back together later."

The ceramics aren't in pieces—they are in *shards*. The sharp, pointy, dusty kind. Glue doesn't stand a chance against this kind of destruction. But what good would it be to point that out when Darcy's so visibly upset?

"Let me help," I say again, softer.

This time she hands me the dustpan and starts dutifully sweeping the last pieces inside.

"I can't get cut," the young guy in the shop tells us. "Blood makes me faint."

I know him from gym class, I realize. Kyle Something.

Kyle *Holtzenberg*.

Darcy mentioned the Holtzenbergs when we stood together on Fableview Boulevard. The way she'd said their last name made them sound annoying. She painted an effective picture, because if Kyle's gym-class-hero behavior is anything to go off of, he definitely lives up to that legacy.

Whispering so as to intentionally exclude Kyle, I tell Darcy, "We don't have to pass out the cards if you're not up for it."

"Of course I'm up for it." There it is again, that challenge. The need to prove something to me that's already been proven.

"My aunt will be tagging along," I say, trying to communicate with my eyes that I know this is weird and I am very sorry, but it cannot be avoided.

This is Aunt Cal's version of mentorship—lurking.

"Cool," Darcy says. She looks to Cal and waves at her. "Nice to officially meet you. I'm Darcy. I've seen you around Fableview, of course. I love your quilt coat."

Aunt Cal only smiles in response. Not a very friendly one either. It's a worst-case-scenario response, and there is no apologizing for it or explaining her vow of silence.

"Let me just drop this off in the supply closet. Then I'll run up and grab one of my parents to watch the shop," Darcy says.

Once Darcy gets upstairs, it's just me, Cal, and Kyle Holtzenberg inside Pam's Paints.

"Nobody's manning the desk right now. What if one of us stole something?" Kyle asks while Darcy's gone. "That would be funny."

I can't imagine what's funny about that, and neither can Cal, so we unite in our power of glaring, focusing all the intensity onto Kyle.

"I wasn't actually gonna do it." He holds up his hands like he might've already pocketed a ceramic figurine. "I've known Darcy longer than you have anyway. We're kind of dating."

This is a genuine shock. One, for the distinct lack of romantic energy that Kyle and Darcy emanate. I've only been in their shared presence for a few minutes, and it's as flat as a carbonated drink left out on a counter for too long. Two, anytime I've ever had the misfortune of getting placed on Kyle's dodgeball team in gym or asked to pair up for badminton, he is annoying. Ruthlessly competitive at eight in the morning, when the rest of us are barely awake.

And three, I guess I hoped Darcy would have not necessarily *higher* standards but different ones. She doesn't have to like girls. I would never believe she could like me.

But Kyle Holtzenberg?

When Darcy comes down the stairs, any trace of her previous crying is gone. She's smiling with all her teeth, as usual. There's a fresh coat of lip gloss on her mouth, shiny and pink and perfect. Her mom follows, dressed in the same fifties costume she wore at the paint lesson.

Aunt Cal darts outside. She is so precise in her movements that she manages to open the door without activating the bell chime. If Darcy is part of a legacy protector family, what does Darcy's mom know about my family? What does Cal know about Darcy's?

"Our newest committee member," Mrs. Keller says, waving at me.

"Yes," I say.

"*You* joined the planning committee?" Kyle asks, using the same voice that comes out whenever I manage to score a basket in gym class or whatever.

"Of course I did." I narrow my eyes in the exact way I know freaks him out. He's so confident in my inability to do anything that it weirdly makes me braver. "Are you not a member?"

"My parents are," he says.

"*Hmm.*"

"See you in a bit!" Darcy calls out to her mom.

"Love you, sweetie," her mom calls back. "Enjoy the parade!"

Out on Fableview Boulevard, the sidewalk is lined with the barrier ropes that Darcy discussed at the meeting. Kids in costumes trot proudly down the middle of the street, beaming at the spectators. Though my clothes are black—and so is my heart—even I think this parade is adorable.

"I'm gonna head out," Kyle tells us.

Darcy waves goodbye. Kyle lifts a single hooked finger in response, then saunters off in the other direction.

"Thank god." Darcy sounds so relieved to be free of him that I can't help but smile. Even if she is dating him, at least she knows it's a joy to see him leave. That's progress I can get behind.

Spectators stand right up against the ropes. It's easy for us to get around, so long as we hug close to the shops.

"Did that wizard man ever get his parade ropes fixed?" I ask Darcy.

"That's Mr. Breck," Darcy tells me. "He didn't even check, so I went over there on Wednesday after school and looked myself. I brought him his replacements this morning."

I want to comment on how she seems to juggle, like, eight different balls in the air at any given moment, but she's been defensive every time I've tried to let her know I see her, and the last thing I want is to be another problem on her list.

"It's a very tight-knit community," I say instead, thinking again of her mom and Aunt Cal. Her mom looks older than Cal, but surely they know each other, even if Darcy's mom doesn't know Cal is a witch, or doesn't believe she's a real one.

"Definitely," Darcy confirms, "The locals tend to stick around for a long time. Their whole lives, usually."

"Can't relate," I say.

Darcy laughs. There it is again. My own little trophy. "Yeah, I've been wanting to ask you. Where did you live before you came here?"

I steal a glance back at Cal, who walks about fifteen feet behind us. "Oh, I've lived all over. My family has a . . . community philosophy on raising children. They want each kid to experience new things, so we live with a different relative every year or two of our lives until we turn eighteen."

"That's *so* cool," Darcy says. It's the opposite reaction to how most people receive this. Not that I've shared it in years. But the general response is usually *What*, with a dozen spiritual question marks afterward.

Probably because I can't share the *real* reason. We train with as many members of our extended family as possible to enhance our powers, learning different tips and tricks and hopefully deepening our own understanding of our magic in the process. We also get to experience various towns that have already been exposed to magic, with the idea being to choose one as our landing spot after our initiations. We meet and make friends with all the wonderful people who live in these places, recruiting one of them for our protection.

Quiet, sullen Aunt Cal *chose* to live in Fableview. She picked this place with its paper cutouts of bedsheet ghosts in every store window and a bronzed broomstick in the middle of the town square. Aunt Cal, the loner, chose a place that loves gathering for group activities. And she picked a person here to protect her.

His name is on the tip of my tongue. It was a man, that much I know. Someone she was not just friends with, but in love with. And he screwed her over. Which makes for the only additional rule Cal has ever given me, on top of the general one that goes for all Doyle witches, saying we are never to mess with the natural order of human life, which basically boils down to *don't use your powers to stop death.*

Cal's rule was much more specific. More pointed.

*Never let your protector be a romantic interest.*

Darcy Keller was crossed off my list from the moment I first saw her.

Losing my powers should be making me increasingly worried, but somehow, the further this goes, the more it feels like a relief. How the people of Fableview live—the mortal people, that is—there *is* something charming about it. They enjoy Halloween because it's fun to dress up in different costumes and put plastic skeletons in their front yards. They make being a witch seem exciting, even to me, who has only ever seen my gift as a burden.

They make me believe it will all work out.

# 9

# DARCY

"By the way, what's happening with the shop?" Anya asks now that we're far enough down the boulevard that Pam's Paints is no longer in sight. "Did you make a decision about whether or not you're going to take it over?"

"Yeah, I'm going to do it. Which reminds me, we should pass these out." I hand her the cards I had printed. "It's a mini scavenger hunt. If a tourist goes into five different shops on the boulevard and posts a picture online inside each one, they get 30 percent off their purchase at Pam's Paints."

Anya reads over the details, and a slow grin creeps across her face. Her smile is as secretive as the rest of her, not easily earned. It's a little thrill to know I've caused it.

"This is great," she says. "You'll get people posting, and then they'll buy something at your shop. It's really well-considered. Do your parents know?"

"Of course they don't know," I tell her, trying for a breeziness that isn't landing, still stuck on everything I revealed to her that first night she showed up at the shop. It's hard to explain that that was only a momentary weakness. "By the time anyone completes this, I should be back at Pam's, finishing up my shift. My parents never check our receipts very closely, so they won't know about the discount. Hopefully, they'll just see the uptick in business and be thrilled. And maybe the other shops will see what we've done and want to offer their own discounts next year. If I'm lucky, it will come up at next year's planning meeting like it's a tradition we've always honored that they just forgot about. That's one big perk of having older parents. You can make them think they forgot something you never said in the first place."

Anya nods. "Risky. I like it. What happened with the dog painting thing, though? Were your parents mad at you?"

"My parents don't really get mad at me," I say. "They get *disappointed*. They gave me a long speech where they asked me not to betray them again." I try to laugh, but the sound is too choked to seem real.

Anya looks at the card, reading through it again. "You really want to own Pam's Paints next year?"

Being around her reminds me of a sleepless night, the kind when suddenly you can see ten years into your own past with clarity, running through every memory you've ever had, piecing your life together like a puzzle. She makes me feel alert, aware of myself and my decisions in a way I never am around anyone else. She doesn't let me get away with my usual easy avoidances, and I don't entirely know what to do with that.

It helps a bit that her aunt lurks behind us, watching our every movement. It's like an extra layer of protection, keeping me from needing to go to the depths that Anya seems to want to take me to. Being around her, I want to say things like *Actually, before I broke those ceramics, I wanted to leave. No one knows that, not even Grace. I even applied to one college already, just as an experiment. Only to see if I could get in.*

The very things I cannot be saying, not now, when my parents have publicly pledged the shop to me. Not when I've accepted without protest. Not when I know things will break without me, and no one else will know how to fix them.

"I do," I tell her.

The lack of conviction in my voice is obvious to us both, and she lets out a small "Hmm" before dropping it altogether. She hands me back half the stack of cards, and we begin passing them out.

As we go down the boulevard, I help Anya identify the tourists, and we approach them with the cards. Once you know what to look for, they're pretty easy to spot. They're always just a little bit in the way, not thinking about the flow of Fableview in the way the locals do. And they tend to take double the pictures of a normal person. Young Fableview kids participate in the parade too, but it isn't the same banner spectacle that it is for a tourist's family.

When we spot a smiling couple waiting for their kid to pass—phones out to take multiple pictures of the tree nearest them—Anya and I exchange a glance, knowing this is our next target.

"Hello," Anya says to them, surprising me by initiating the conversation before I can. "Would you like to perform a scavenger hunt that results in a discount from a local business?" It's her first time asking this instead of me, and the stiff formality in her tone almost makes me laugh. But she's trying, for *me*, and I would never dare mock her for that.

"That sounds fun," the woman says warmly. "How lovely. Thank you!"

Anya nods. "Of course." She walks off.

"That was perfect," I tell her.

"It was a start." She wipes away the hint of a smile that had crept into her expression.

*"Don't,"* I say, almost reaching for her face.

"Don't what?"

"I just . . . I like when you smile, is all," I say.

After about an hour, I'm out of cards, and so is Anya. We've stopped to watch the parade. It's an endless stream of young kids in costumes, smiling and waving and begging for candy.

Grace spots me.

"Hey, bitch," she says, grinning. She has on a disco ball minidress, sparkling silver tights, and matching silver boots. One of her tamer looks. It's too early in October for her to bust out the more elaborate costumes in her collection. She notices Anya and immediately straightens up. "We use that term affectionately. It's our love language. It's kind of like a subversion of sorts. You wouldn't understand."

"I understand perfectly," Anya says, her stare unflinching.

Grace half laughs, giving me one quick, urgent glance.

"Anya's been helping me pass out these scavenger hunt cards, since *someone* didn't want to be involved," I say. Grace literally screamed when I told her my plan, then started holding up the sign of the cross, telling me she'd rather swim in a pool of sharks than betray my parents with this scheme.

"Hmm," she says now, tapping her chin. "That person sounds really gorgeous and smart. Probably the most interesting, intelligent person you know."

"Probably," I respond. "Where's Maddie?" Maddie is Grace's four-year-old sister. The youngest Manalo, and the only one in their family still participating in the Fableview parade.

"My mom just texted, saying Maddie should be coming around the corner soon. She's dressed as a manananggal. My mom wouldn't let her be too scary with it, though. She was afraid it would freak out the other little kids. So she just kind of looks like Dracula with wings."

Grace's whole family is Filipino, and I know from her that the manananggal is sort of the Filipino folklore equivalent to a vampire but much gorier. A few months ago, Maddie snuck out of her room and watched a horror movie with Grace and their thirteen-year-old sister, Claire. Ever since then, Maddie has become obsessed with scary stuff. She was begging for something scary to sleep with at night, so her mom got her a teddy bear that had stitch marks across its eyes and mouth. But even that wasn't enough for Maddie. So Grace brought Maddie to the art shop. Maddie and I picked out some paints and random scrap materials, and we covered her teddy in fake blood and sewed on oozing organs made of felt. It was genuinely grotesque-looking. Grace says Maddie drags it everywhere in the house now, completely obsessed.

That's the kind of thing I love most about working at the art shop—getting to help other people make their creative visions come to life.

Maddie appears, tiny and always a little disheveled, her long black hair in tangles I can see even from here. There's blood spattered across her light brown skin, and huge plastic fangs poke out of her mouth, with large, bat-like wings perched on her small back.

She is sobbing.

When she sees Grace, she runs over to her. "Look!" She turns to the side, showing Grace where the fabric on her wings has ripped. "It got stuck on a tree!" Her crying turns into big, dramatic sobs again as Grace wraps her in a hug.

"Maddie, you look amazing," I tell her. "I never would've noticed that."

"You're just saying that to make me feel better," she tells me, snot rockets falling onto Grace's shoulders.

I *am* just saying it to make her feel better, so she's got me there.

"Can I look at it?" Anya asks.

There's something about Anya that makes Maddie stop crying almost instantly. Maybe it's her stillness. She never makes you feel rushed, or even worried. Or it could be the warmth of her eyes. There's an unmistakable, inviting gentleness there.

Maddie stares at Anya in the way only a four-year-old can, with unshielded curiosity, patiently making her own judgment call.

She releases her hold on Grace and walks up to Anya, deciding to trust her.

I want to ask Grace if she still thinks Anya is sinister, but this moment is too fragile for all that.

"I'm really good at fixing things," Anya tells Maddie, holding the broken part of the wing in her hands. "I think I can put this back together."

Still awestruck, Maddie takes the wings off her shoulders.

Anya turns her back to all of us, huddling in the corner. Less than thirty seconds later, she spins around again. And somehow, the wings are good as new. The fine, gauzelike fabric shows no trace of a rip. There isn't even a seam.

"How did you do that?" I ask.

"What? That literally took you, like, twenty-three seconds," Grace overlaps, her jaw hanging open.

"YouTube tutorials," Anya deadpans. She squats down to help get the wing straps back around Maddie's shoulders.

Maddie throws her arms around Anya for a big, fat, four-year-old hug.

Grace gives me another look, and I genuinely wish I'd asked about the sinister thing, because this isn't sinister at all.

But it *is* something strange.

The kind of strange everyone talks about in Fableview. What others would say is almost . . . magical.

But I know there's more to it. Anya Doyle has tricks up her sleeve, like the novelty coins I carry in the pocket of my witch costume.

Aunt Cal closes in on us. She says nothing, just steps closer and closer until she places a hand on Anya's forearm and starts to tug.

"I have to go," Anya tells me. "I'm really sorry. I'll be at Monday's planning meeting. I think? I hope."

"It's okay if you can't make it!" I call out as Cal hustles Anya away from me. "But we'd love to have you at the pumpkin patch party on Wednesday!"

Maddie returns to the parade, and Grace and I find spots along the barrier to watch her continue marching on, happy as ever now, catching candy from spectators.

"That sort of seemed, like . . . *magical*," Grace whispers. It's a genuine whisper too, which is how I know she's serious. She doesn't want to be overheard, so she speaks through gritted teeth.

"Obviously it wasn't magical," I respond with my normal voice. There's nothing to whisper about. "That night outside the shop, I told her how none of the so-called magic here is real. I joked that people learn tricks from YouTube tutorials. That's why she said that. And that's probably where she learned how to do that too."

"Okay . . . But, like, the wings were in *perfect* condition," Grace says. "I know you don't believe the witches here are real— and that's fine, I can't prove it either—but that seemed kind of impossible to do without some sort of power."

"Maybe she's a speed seamstress," I say.

"Is that a thing?"

"Probably. Everything's a thing."

"Okay, well then, I changed my mind. You have to figure out what is going on with her," Grace tells me. "Because I'd bet my life that you're becoming friends with a real-life witch."

"I bet my life that I'm not," I say, turning back to catch one last glimpse of Anya before she disappears into the crowd. "And I'll find a way to prove it to you."

# 16 Days Until Halloween

# 10

# ANYA

My actions at the costume parade were not enough to break Cal's vow of silence. We stayed silent on our ride home, and then Cal left me alone in the house for the rest of the night. I thought she would never bring it up again, but when I asked if I could go to the pumpkin patch party—whatever *that* is—she surprised me by saying yes. *Nodding* yes, more like it, and then writing down that my "little magic stunt" at the costume parade was "entirely irrational" and "seemed to be motivated by romantic feelings, which should be avoided at all costs when choosing a protector for the upcoming initiation."

I still don't know why I fixed Maddie's wings. She was just looking so sad, and I knew I could do something about it. There aren't any official rules about practicing magic in public. Obviously the whole town of Fableview relies on the belief that real witches live here. But if Darcy's right about anything, it's that the true magic is in the mystery. I know better than anyone that making the exact nature of my powers known to too many mortals starts to make them want things from me that I can't accomplish. They don't care about who I am as a person, only what I can give to them.

Fixing Maddie's costume may be one of my last acts as a mender.

What I do need is to make a real plan for my nonwitch life. I've got to learn how regular people choose their passions. Make their money. All of it.

As seems to be the case with every event in Fableview, today's pumpkin patch party is very on theme. There are pumpkins *everywhere*. Real ones, stuffed ones, paintings of ones. Families roam the patch of actual pumpkins, walking up and down rows, searching for the perfect ones to buy. There are booths full of pumpkin-themed foods. And lots of people dressed in appropriately pumpkin-esque clothing.

I pass countless classmates, making a promise to myself that if anyone makes eye contact with me, I will try to make an honest effort to talk to them in return. Without the weight of worrying about whether they can be my protector, maybe it will be easier to make a real friend.

If there's one thing I have going for me today, it's that Aunt Cal has decided not to attend, writing that she found it "emotionally exhausting to trail teenagers." But I guess the same could be said for everyone else. They don't have strange, reclusive witch aunts who wear patchwork quilt jackets and take vows of silence that even social customs cannot break. In a month, I won't have that either. I won't have anything, actually.

That's when I see the flash of red hair, the shock of curls that can sometimes wake me from a dead sleep.

*Julia.*

There's no way it's her, so many years after we last saw each other, hundreds of miles from here. Then again, a lot of the people in Fableview are tourists, and Halloween was always Julia's favorite holiday. The year we were supposedly friends, we wore matching costumes on Halloween. We were green M&M's. Her choice. She wanted us to be the same, and while I wouldn't ordinarily want to dress as a green M&M, I was thrilled to be included. I happily wore the costume with her.

Now I look back and I know it wasn't about wanting us to dress alike because we were best friends. It was about wanting to see how much control she had over me. In the end, I'm glad she didn't have all of it.

She's a year older than I am, so she'd be out of high school by now. She could take a spontaneous October trip if she wanted. And what better place for a Halloween enthusiast than Fableview?

Possessed by something—a need to know for sure, a desire for closure, maybe all of it—I chase down those curls. I'm a wrecking ball, crashing into strollers, bumping shoulders with my classmates.

"Doyle!" someone calls out.

Doyle is *my* last name, but I have never been the type of person to go by it, so I continue on my path.

"Um, hello?"

Grace Manalo steps in front of me, waving a corn on the cob in my face. She's dressed as a jack-o'-lantern, wearing a long orange dress with a smiling black face on her stomach and a stem hat on her head. It's an outfit that would look ridiculous on anyone else, but on Grace, it somehow seems understated, even with the false orange eyelashes she wears.

"I know you heard me say your name." She takes a huge bite of corn, unmoved by the startled urgency in my eyes. "I don't trust you," she continues, forcing my attention off the crowd and onto her. "Ever since you moved here, you just kind of *lurk* everywhere you go. Which is weird already, but you do it in this way where it's like you're more mysterious than the rest of us. And I'm kind of tired of it."

"I'm sorry," I say. The longer we speak, the farther away the red curls get in the crowd. "I really have to go."

"I don't have the capacity for another brooding mystery around here." Grace puts her corncob up to block my exit. "Ask anyone what happened with me and Parker Holt last year. They ruined my life with their brooding. It was such a production. When we went to the Fall Ball together, they didn't get me a corsage. Which is actually fine, because I'm really picky, and I wouldn't have worn it if it didn't go with my dress. But it *did* hurt my feelings. Sometimes it's about the gesture, not the actual result. I needed to know they cared enough to look for something for me. That's all. And, by the way, I'm not even, like, attracted to you. Not that you're unattractive. Don't read into this. It's just, on an energy level, I think I would devour you in a way that wouldn't be fun for either of us. I have no interest in someone who can't match me."

At some point, Grace's rate of speaking slowed down. She's talking at an almost comical pace, like someone has put her audio on half speed. The red curls are fully out of sight, and I am standing still, strangely transfixed by this speech Grace is giving.

"I'm legitimately afraid you're going to ruin my life through proximity." She takes a full ten seconds to hit every syllable. "Like, you're the type who would substitute almond milk for regular milk in my latte. It would be very bad. I'd have to use my EpiPen."

"If you have a nut allergy, I will never give you something with nuts in it," I tell her.

"That's it?" Her regular rate of speech returns. "You don't have anything else to say to all that?"

"Not really. Could you show me who Parker Holt is, though? I've heard the name, but I can't put a face to them right now."

"Search the crowd for the person who looks like they could inflict the most possible emotional damage on you."

I can't tell if she's joking, so I do search the crowd. It's a good excuse to give one last scan for the red hair.

I spot Darcy instead. The clouds have parted, and there she stands, shining like the sun in her pumpkin sweater and matching headband, smiling as she puts a pumpkin sticker onto a little kid's shirt.

"I was kidding. Parker isn't here," Grace says. "Unless maybe they are." She pulls out her phone, scanning through her pictures in a panic until she finds one to show me. "This is them, okay? If you see them, you need to warn me."

"You just said they're *not* here," I remind her, looking at a blurry black-and-white photo of a person in silhouette. I couldn't recognize Parker Holt if I tried.

"Things can change, Doyle," Grace says. "Please keep up."

Darcy makes her way over to us, squeezing Grace's shoulder. "Please tell me you're reminding people about the face painting." Then she looks at me and says in a voice so gentle it makes my neck tingle, "Hey."

"Where did you set up for it?" I ask, working very hard not to make too much of the honey-sweet change in her tone.

"I'm doing it in the Pam's Paints booth. My parents are spending the day leading pumpkin carving demos on the main stage, so they won't see me over there."

"Smart."

"I thought you'd know where to find me, but then I remembered you haven't been to the pumpkin patch party before. Do you want to see our booth?"

"I'll come check it out in a bit," Grace answers, not realizing the question is for me. "I'm running a perimeter check for Parker."

"Sounds good." Darcy sticks her hand out. "Here, come with me."

When I grab on, there are a dozen zaps in the center of my chest, tiny fireworks of excitement that bounce off my sternum. Darcy Keller is guiding me through this crowd of locals and tourists. She's holding my hand.

"I love the pumpkin patch party," she says.

"What exactly makes it a party?"

Darcy laughs. She appreciates my dry observations, which is why I've started making them more. Just to keep winning at my own contest. And to be considerate of her feelings. She likes to laugh, and I seem to be able to provide that for her. It's the least I can do for the kindness she's shown me.

"I guess it's not really. Although, anything can be a party if you believe hard enough," she says. "This is just an excuse to pick pumpkins. Every event in Fableview has a fun official name that's long and silly. That's one thing I *wouldn't* change."

"Are you sure? It's tough to tell people I'm at the"—I glance at the sign overhead—"Playfully Picturesque Pumpkin Patch Party.

What with the reputation I've gained for being brooding and mysterious."

"Grace told you," Darcy says, scandalized.

"She did," I say.

"Please don't let her get to you. Grace has a knack for . . . exaggerating."

"She's correct, though. Nobody knows me. And I'm usually melancholic. Though hopefully I won't destroy her life like Parker Holt did."

Darcy glances over her shoulder. *"Please* don't say their name. They're like Beetlejuice. Three mentions and they really do appear."

We pass Kyle Holtzenberg participating in what looks to be some form of pumpkin bowling. He clocks me, and I clock him right back, remembering what he said in the shop about how he and Darcy were "kind of dating." He doesn't look worried that Darcy's holding my hand, which sparks my competitive energy. I don't know if he *should* be worried—I have no idea if Darcy isn't straight—but it would be nice for Kyle to know the world doesn't revolve around his appeal.

We arrive at the Pam's Paints booth, currently guarded by nothing more than a sign that says BE RIGHT BACK. It's charming but strange, the amount of trust everyone has around here. I'd say I want to learn how to adopt it for myself, but Kyle's probably pocketed at least three handcrafted figurines in Darcy's absence.

When I'm mortal, I will still lock my doors at night.

"Your parents really won't see this?" I ask Darcy, gesturing to the face paint supplies.

"They usually stay inside the barn the whole time," she says. "They're kind of like the mayors of Halloween here."

"I've picked up on that."

*"Yeah."* She's careful not to put too much friction into it, but there's still just enough unrest there to let me know she's annoyed. "I end up doing a lot of the actual day-to-day work for all our events because they're so busy overseeing the big picture. Which I guess is what I'll be doing next year. Although, knowing them, they'll still be doing it with me. But for now, they won't have any idea I'm the secret face painter. Unless they recognize my handiwork. In which case, I'll apologize when they tell me how disappointed they are, and I will do a better job of hiding my artistic flair next time."

"You know, you deserve whatever it is you want out of life," I say. "Even if it's *not* to be the next Halloween mayor of Fableview."

Darcy fumbles her face painting brushes, flustered. "You're very kind for someone who completely ignored me the first two times I ever tried talking to you."

I've hoped for many things when it comes to Darcy Keller, but few have been stronger than my hope that she didn't remember those moments. That gazing into her eyes, smelling the cloud of strawberry-and-vanilla perfume as she'd whipped her head around to face me, I'd lost my ability to do even the bare minimum level of speaking.

"I'm really sorry," I tell her.

"Was I rude to you or something?"

"No," I hurry out. "I just get shy around pretty girls."

Now it's *my* turn to fumble. The truth's fallen out without any consideration for my audience—the pretty girl who makes me shy. I'm folding inside myself, hoping to become so small and insignificant, she forgets to notice I'm here. Maybe even forgets my existence at all.

"Oh" is all she says, worsening the effect.

A hollow silence falls over the tent. Never in my life did I think I'd be grateful for the presence of Kyle Holtzenberg, but when he struts up to the tent, yelling, *"Daaaaaaaarce,"* it is a balm to my blackened soul.

He's accompanied by another classmate of ours. She was in my math class last year, and she's a part of Darcy's social circle when she's around, which isn't all that often.

"Piper! Welcome back," Darcy says, springing up to hug her, completely ignoring Kyle. And also me. Lots of ignoring going on around this tent.

There it is. Piper Blake.

Her hair is as red as Julia's, though it's not curly, so there's no chance she was the person I saw earlier. Piper's is pulled back into a thick braid, round-rimmed glasses perched on her nose. The tiny pumpkin embroidered on her collared shirt matches the one stitched into the front pocket of her dark green corduroy pants. Where Darcy and Grace's passion for dressing on theme is loud and bright, Piper's seems as tidy and contained as she is.

"Sorry I missed the costume parade," Piper says. "I hope it went well."

"It was great," Darcy tells her. "This is Anya, by the way."

"Hi," I say.

"We had math together last year."

"We did," I confirm.

"Darcy's been hanging out with Anya a lot," Kyle interjects.

A shot of something—adrenaline or a last-ditch effort not

to die of mortification—straightens my spine. "Aren't you and Darcy kind of dating?" I ask Kyle.

Darcy gasps. "Did he say that? We're *not* dating. I'm very, very single."

"Yeah, Darcy says she'd never date someone in Fableview," Kyle tells me. "But if she would, it would probably be me. Which is what I meant. I just didn't get a chance to explain that the other day, because I was too busy making sure all the ceramic pieces got cleaned up."

"I wouldn't *never* date someone," Darcy says.

Now, *this* is interesting. Everyone has something to prove, except Piper Blake, who leans against a tent leg, smiling. "I think I missed a lot more than the costume parade," she says.

# 11

## DARCY

*What's happening right now?*

Somehow, this has turned into a conversation about who is dating who.

No one is dating anyone.

"Everything is *fine*," I say. There's a child standing twenty feet away. I spring up to approach her and her guardian. "Would you like your face painted? It's free!"

It's actually ten dollars, but I need a task more than I need the money, so this one will be on the house.

Anya told me she gets shy around pretty girls, and now I'm shy around her. It's not like me to be shy. It's also not like me to miss someone's interest in me. It's *also* not like me to rebel against my parents this much.

Or maybe all of it is like me. Maybe it's just been easier to ignore it because my entire life, I've been taught to fear change. That there's no use in tweaking what's already working. But the truth is, everything changes anyway. It's harder to stop it from happening than it is to embrace it.

The random child does not want a free face painting, so I text Grace and ask her if Maddie's here. Grace responds within seconds, confirming her whole family is in attendance.

**Send Maddie over to our booth, I write. I'll paint her face for free. And you should come too. I need help. I'll explain later.**

**Coming.**

Grace is outside the booth by the time I've slowly walked myself back. The swell of gratitude I feel for her is so overwhelming, I have to give her a hug.

"Thank you for always showing up for me," I say.

"Wow, it's that bad?" she asks, giving my back hard, confused pats.

"It'll all be fine," I say.

*"Cryptic."*

If Anya, Kyle, and Piper have held a conversation in my absence, that's not for me to know. No one's moved from the position I left them in, that's for sure.

"I understand now," Grace says to me upon entering the tent. She gives Piper a hug. "Did you just get back?"

"This morning," Piper tells her. "We have *a lot* to catch up on." She gives a meaningful look at Anya, who diverts her gaze by arranging my face painting supplies.

She's started putting the brushes in order from thinnest to thickest. It's a really sweet gesture. Something I'd planned to do myself but hadn't gotten around to yet. It's very cute.

*She's* very cute.

My internal panic button goes off, repeating *Oh my god* with increased urgency. Anya does have a brooding mysteriousness.

But there is also this thoughtfulness about her. The measured actions, like arranging my brushes the way I would. Her eyes have this half-open thing about them where she's always looking a little skeptical or sleepy. And she's got a downturned mouth. I used to think it was because she was always a little sad. But she's not. She's just selective with her trust. Her joy. When something rare infects her with it, it's like watching the string lights turn on for the first night of October, sparkling and wonderful.

The rest of Grace's family arrives. Maddie sees Anya and gives her a big squeeze. Anya is bewildered at first, unprepared for the affection.

But then it happens. The string light effect. She glows from top to bottom, hugging Maddie back.

"Are you getting your face painted?" Anya asks.

"I don't think so," Maddie says.

"Yes, she is," Mrs. Manalo interjects. She looks to Maddie. "That's why we came over here."

"But I don't want to anymore," Maddie protests, tears already welling.

"We can do whatever you want," I say, squatting down so I can get on Maddie's level. My parents have always encouraged me to do this with young kids. So they see me as an equal. "But it's also okay if you don't want to."

Maddie shifts from foot to foot.

"She told me this morning she wanted to be a butterfly," Mrs. Manalo offers up. She has a bag slung over her shoulder and a tired look on her face. "I don't know what changed."

"No, I didn't!" Maddie protests. The tears start spilling over. "I don't like butterflies."

"I told you, you don't have to like only scary things," Grace says. "You can like butterflies too. Like me. I love reptiles and glitter. It's a family tradition at this point. And Darcy's *really* good at painting. She can make you into whatever kind of butterfly you want."

She's as good at convincing Maddie to do things as she is at convincing me. It must be her perfect big-sister voice—confident but also gentle. You trust what she's saying, which makes you want to trust yourself.

"Even a scary one," I add, even though I'm not sure what that would look like.

"I don't like butterflies!" Maddie insists. With this doubling down, her face has gone from red to purple. The tears turn into choking sobs as she repeats her insistence that she never, not once, mentioned wanting to be a butterfly.

Kyle flees the scene, mumbling something about needing a turkey leg. Piper slinks off too, as is her way, never really holding to one person or place for very long.

"She definitely did," Claire says. She always finds a way to escalate the trouble. "It's fine if you changed your mind, but you for sure said it."

"We can paint you into anything you want, Maddie," I remind her.

This situation has certainly taken the attention away from Anya and me, but I'm not sure that it's any less stressful.

"Sometimes I get embarrassed when I'm the only one doing something," Anya says. Her voice is so quiet that it takes a second for all of us to realize she's talking to the group. "But I'd feel a lot better about getting my face painted if you did it too."

Maddie looks up from the ground. Her eyes, wrung red and watery, widen.

"I was thinking about being a butterfly too," Anya continues. "Do you think that's a good idea? I'm not sure I can pull it off. I only wear black. I'm kind of scared other people will think I look really silly with a butterfly on my face. They probably think I should have spiders there. Maybe we could be butterflies together? That would really help me."

Maddie doesn't even hesitate when she says, "Okay." Her tears stop completely, and she plops into the open chair, her tiny legs swinging as she waits for me to begin.

The rest of the Manalo family is stunned into silence.

"I'm great at butterflies," I tell Maddie, dampening my pastel watercolors. "What color should we make yours?"

"Pink," she says emphatically.

I turn to Anya and my breath hitches. Suddenly I can't remember how to be calm around her. There's this tingling, uncapturable feeling inside me. I'm a butterfly too.

"Do you want me to make yours dark?" I ask.

"No way," she says, more to Maddie than to me. "I want pink too."

"Two pink butterflies, coming right up," I say.

I paint Maddie's face first, doing light pink wings over her eyes and cheeks and a dark pink butterfly body up her nose, with dark pink accents all around. She blows hot breath in my face, snot still crusted around the edge of her nose. But she's calm, her long lashes pressed into the tops of her cheeks because she's keeping her eyes closed for the entire process.

When I'm done, I pull out the mirror from under my seat

to show her, and she beams at herself in open adoration. "I'm a *butterfly*!" she says, delighted. She jumps out of the chair as quickly as she jumped in it. "Let's go get our pumpkins!" she tells her mom and sisters.

"Don't you want to see your friend's face get painted?" Mrs. Manalo asks.

Maddie looks back at Anya. "You can show me when you're done," she says with finality, skipping off toward the pumpkin patch.

Mrs. Manalo tries to slip me a twenty, but I refuse. "I insist," she says, a naked urgency in her eyes. "That was magic."

"It was," I say, looking again at Anya.

"Thanks for that," Grace says once her mom and sisters are out of earshot.

"No problem," Anya tells her.

"I'd stick around, but you've put my mom in a good mood, and I want to use that to my advantage by convincing her to buy me something fun."

When Anya and I are alone, I plunge forward with my painting task with way too much aggression, nearly poking Anya's eye out with hot pink paint.

"Sorry," I say, my hands shaking.

"That was my bad," she tells me. "I'll do a better job of holding still."

She leans forward. Having just spent twenty minutes with a four-year-old mouth breathing on me, it's a much different experience with Anya's face so close to mine. I can see the flecks of rich honey in her brown eyes. Her lips have vertical lines creasing in the middle that I have this overwhelming urge to paint. Not with my face painting watercolors. Onto a canvas. With oil, maybe. Such a difficult medium. So time-consuming. So complex.

My portraiture has never been very good, but these are lips I'd need to practice at anyway, getting the bow just right. And those downturned ends. It would be hard not to make them look like a frown. I'd need to find a way to communicate that her mind is moving faster than her mouth can, and she's holding back a thousand interesting thoughts that I want to climb inside her head and learn.

I swipe dark pink down the bridge of her nose, memorizing the way the brush flicks along the curve.

"Thanks for painting my face," she says.

"Your plan all along."

"That's why I joined the Fableview Fall Planning Committee. To be turned into a pink butterfly."

"I knew it."

"About earlier—" she says.

"Don't worry about it," I interrupt, swirling water through the lighter pink, then beginning the wings, drawing the rough outline across her right temple and down to her cheekbones. My heart races, galloping in circles like it's caged, desperate to be set free. "I think you're pretty too."

There. I said it back.

It's not a big deal.

Right?

Except now my hand has decided to shake even harder than before, and Anya's portrait of stillness has cracked too. There's a ghost of a smile on her face, twitching against my brush.

It's very cute.

*She's* very cute.

Whatever.

I'm a professional.

"So what's your—" I start, right as she says, "Have you changed your—" Our words crash into each other like we're blindfolded, roaming around for a safe topic.

"You go," I say. The brush zags in my hand, streaking her cheek with too much pink. "Sorry."

"I don't mind."

I dip a paper towel into my fresh cup of water, reminding myself to breathe. I've been around pretty girls before. It's never been a reason to panic.

"I was going to ask if you've changed your mind yet about owning the paint shop," Anya says.

Her insistence makes me laugh. "You're really convinced I don't want that."

"I am," she confirms.

"Okay, let's say you're right," I say. "Hypothetically. How would I even begin to tell my parents? You saw how they reacted to the dog painting. And I've been doing all these little things, like sneaking the discount cards and offering face painting. They're so busy with their own obligations that they don't even notice the tiny havoc I'm wreaking. All this is nothing compared to telling them I've already applied to a college out of state."

Real excitement bursts forth, jostling Anya forward right as I've just finished wiping off my previous mistake. "You have?"

"*Shh.*" I press my finger to her lips to quiet her down. And maybe to feel them. For the sake of my future art, of course. "Yes. Just one. I used my work money to pay for the application. I won't get in, so I don't think it matters yet anyway. It's just an experiment, I guess."

"Of course you'll get in," she says. "Vous êtes le meilleur élève de notre classe."

"C'est faux!" I protest. *It's false.*

"C'est vrai," she challenges. *It's true.*

"All right, your turn." I turn her face to start the wings on her other cheek. "Tell me something about you no one else knows. Like how you fixed Maddie's wings so fast. Grace insists it was magic. She's convinced you're an actual witch." With my hands on Anya's face, I can feel her teeth clench together. "You don't have to," I throw out, not wanting to lose our progress by being too bossy.

The silence swells.

I paint my way through it.

"I'm not a witch," she says. "I'm just a regular person."

The strangest thing happens. Her answer disappoints me. It's not as crushing as it was when I was younger and my parents sat me down to tell me the truth about every other magical thing in my life. *They* were Santa Claus. *They* were the Easter Bunny. *They* were the tooth fairy.

Anya is just so . . . special, I guess. She really does feel like magic.

I'm about to ask how she did it when she says, "I used to have this friend named Julia."

"No one knows you had a friend named Julia?" I tease, hoping the ribbing sets her further at ease. When her jaw relaxes, I smile a bit to myself.

"No one knows why we stopped being friends," she tells me. "She told everybody it was because I was a bad person."

"What really happened?"

"It's kind of complicated. For a few months, we did everything together. Everything Julia wanted to do, that is. It's easier for me to stay quiet and go along with things."

"I like it when you speak up," I tell her.

"It's easy to talk to you," she tells me.

My paintbrush runs along the hard line of her jaw. I have the strangest urge to touch it with my fingers. The brush isn't enough. "Tell me what happened with Julia," I whisper.

"She asked me to do something impossible. When I told her I couldn't, she told me I was a liar and a horrible person who didn't care about other people. She told everybody else in town the same thing. And because I was so quiet, and she wasn't, they all believed her. It got so bad that I had to cut my time living with that relative short."

Ever since Anya arrived in Fableview, she has been alone. I've never once seen her hang out with anyone or even hold a conversation with a classmate in the hallway. It seemed to be how she wanted things, considering how she treated me in French class. My heart aches, knowing the truth.

I wish I could see pictures of this Julia. Read her social media posts and pass judgment on her. But Anya is so skittish. Scared and delicate and afraid to trust. The last thing I want to do is overwhelm her by asking too much at once.

I decide to say, "That's Julia's loss. You're my favorite person I've met in a really long time. Probably ever."

This close, I can see Anya's pupils dilate, zeroing in on my lips. Goose bumps prickle along my arms. My heart feels like it grows three sizes. All I'm doing is painting a hot pink butterfly on Anya's face, but somehow, I feel completely, totally *alive*.

She doesn't tell me any more about Julia. I paint in silence, each brushstroke another gentle offering to her. A beckoning. *Trust me enough to tell me the rest someday.*

When I finish her face painting, I hand her the mirror to take a look.

"Oh, I don't think I want to know," she tells me, batting the mirror away.

"C'mon! You have to!" I insist. "You look cute!" This time I say it on purpose. It has the same effect on me—that zipping, slippery rush.

She keeps her hand on the mirror.

"I'm really proud of you for applying to a college. I just want you to know that," she tells me.

I promised myself I would never date someone in Fableview.

Yet here I am, kind of wishing I could.

# 14 Days Until Halloween

# 12

# ANYA

As I cower in Aunt Cal's old Volkswagen Beetle—an unfortunate shade of notice-me yellow—my parents initiate their weekly video call. Mom's face crowds the screen, too close to the camera, providing me with an unsolicited tour of her most recent dental work. In the corner, visible only by his shoulder, is my dad.

"We are getting *so* excited!" Mom says.

It would seem my mom's magical power is enthusiasm. Really it's herbalism. In our family, mothers and their firstborn children tend to have complementary powers. It's true for Mom and me. I am best at mending plants. Mom can grow them under almost any condition. When my dad forgot their anniversary a few years ago, she called me to say she'd grown tomatoes in his pillowcase overnight as payback.

"I'm excited too," I tell her, lying through my teeth. The closer their visit gets, the closer I come to having to tell everyone I'm choosing not to join the coven.

"Are you in Cal's car?" Mom asks, spotting the herbs Cal has hanging from her sunroof.

"I'm not driving, though." I flip the camera around to show the view of Fableview Boulevard from where I'm parked. Even through a screen on an overcast day, the charm is clear. If anything, the flat gray sky accentuates the orange of the leaves sprinkled across the cobblestone. It looks like a memory somehow, something that makes me ache with longing for what used to be, even though it's right here, right now.

"Just lovely," Mom says. "I almost chose to live there myself. I'm glad that Cal ended up there."

When I don't see my parents, it's easy to convince myself I don't need them around. I've spent a lot of my life away from them already. But then they're in front of me, even if it's only through a screen, and my chest burns at the thought of giving all this up.

An idea comes to me—a last-ditch shot at finding a loophole that could make my initiation work. "Who is Cal's protector again?" I ask.

Mom leans so close to the phone, I swear it might be inside her mouth. "Oh gosh, I haven't thought about him in years. Mark . . ." Her voice trails off, searching for a last name.

My dad chimes in to answer for her. "Blake."

*Like Piper*, I realize. The Piper who just returned.

"Ah, got it," I say, pretending not to recognize the name. My asking these kinds of questions has already sparked way too much intrigue. It's important I sound bored, like I don't even know why I'm asking. "What happened with Mark and Aunt Cal?"

"He broke her heart into about ten thousand pieces," Mom tells me. "Shattered, I tell you. When he went away to college, he fell in love with another girl. I'm pretty sure that's who he ended up marrying. He didn't tell Cal about her until he came back that summer." Mom squints her eyes. "Why? Did she bring him up?"

"No," I say quickly. "Aunt Cal isn't using words to speak right now."

Mom chuckles. "That sounds like Cal. She reminds me of you in that way. Protective of herself."

"*I talk,*" I protest.

"You sure do." Mom beams. "And I love hearing every single thing you have to say." Sometimes she's so complimentary that there is nowhere to go inside the cage of her kindness.

But I have to press on, searching for a solution. "What happens if you don't talk to your protector anymore? Shouldn't that be grounds for removal the same way it is not to have one at all?"

My mom pulls the camera back. She thinks it will somehow show her more of me instead of show me more of her. I've stepped on a land mine, and it's important to stay still, not making this seem any more interesting than it already is.

"You don't have to speak to someone to have them look out for you. These people take oaths, honey. They're very committed. Mark still follows it, I can promise you that. It's not the same as not having a protector at all."

"What are they even protecting us from? This isn't the 1400s anymore or whatever."

Mom chuckles. "I know, sweetie. It's not. But part of being a witch in our family is about investing in community. And in the event there ever *is* trouble, well then, you have someone you know can look out for you."

"I thought that's what the coven is for," I say.

"It is. But we need more than just our family to thrive, dear. We need other people to witness us. That's all that remains when we're gone. The memories of us that other people carry. That's what really keeps our magic alive. Protectors ensure that too."

Little does she know that in just over two weeks, that's all that will remain of me, even though I'll still be alive and well. Just banished.

"Do protectors have to be mortal?" I ask next. There must be some weak point I can identify. "Actually, could Dad be my protector? He's not in the coven, and he's mortal. He even agreed to take your last name. Feels like he's pretty dedicated to the cause of keeping the magic alive."

"Oh, honey, why are you asking all these questions? You've got yourself a lovely protector! Gosh, I'm getting so excited to meet her. I wish your grandma were still alive to see it. And Darcy's. It's just too special." Mom wipes an actual tear from her eye.

The strange thing about spending so little time actually living with my parents is that they don't know I'm queer. They don't *not* know either. It just isn't something we've discussed when I've stayed with them in the summers or on any of these calls. My identity isn't a thing I have many words for anyway. It just *is*. Like my magic, thrumming through me, always there, even when I'm not accessing it. My queerness makes me who I am, affects every single thing I do, but at the same time, it's only mine to fully know. And I like it that way.

It hasn't occurred to my mom that I might have romantic feelings for Darcy. She assumes Darcy is a safe protector choice because she's a girl.

"I actually have to go," I say. "I'm taking Darcy's ceramics class." This, at least, is true. It's nice to say true things. Even if there are several layers of lies hidden between them.

"Tell her we said hello!" Mom replies. "Love you so much, honey. Can't wait to see you very soon!"

"Love you too."

After hanging up, I take the short walk from my car to Pam's Paints, breathing in that familiar heady scent of impending rain. I feel a huge swell of affection. This place really is lovely. It's a shame I won't be able to stay here either.

Taking in the shops along the boulevard, I look up at the hand-painted signs, thinking of the people who made them, wondering what their stories are. Did they get what they wanted out of life? How did they know who they were meant to become?

The door chime tells Darcy I've arrived. She's back in the same witch's costume from the first night I really spoke to her, only now she's overseeing several tables' worth of people painting ceramics.

It's hard to surprise Darcy Keller. She knows everything about this town. Showing up unannounced has done the trick, and I think I could get addicted to the way her head tilts toward her left shoulder as she places her hand against her heart.

"This wasn't on the schedule," she says in greeting. We've

been clinging to that schedule she gave me, the both of us. At school we say nothing. But if it's an official item on the Fableview October schedule, we're bursting at the seams to talk to each other. There's something unscheduled that I need to do, though. One loose thread that must be fixed before I lose my powers forever.

"I wanted to paint my own ceramic," I say, fighting the urge to stare at the floor, knowing my cheeks are already burning red.

"I'm sorry to say, we haven't made any gnomes in a while."

"That's a real shame."

"I'll tell my parents to order more."

"That will be very appreciated. By me and the gnome community."

"In the meantime, what are you looking to paint?" She directs me to a shelf of unpainted ceramics near the front. "You don't have to do anything Halloween-themed, but we have a good selection right now. Bats, pumpkins, ghosts. *Witches*." She waves her fingers like she's calling back to our long-running joke.

"I'd like to do a cat," I tell her.

This gets a laugh out of her that she doesn't explain, not even when I pry her with my most specific, unflinching, explain-yourself stare.

"Perfect," she says, her sharp green eyes sparkling in delight. "Are cats your favorite?"

"I'm actually allergic. But they say you love what you can't have."

This is supposed to be my attempt at joking right back. The statement has a friction I don't expect. After admitting that I think she's pretty and her telling me the same thing back, electricity has begun humming in the gaps of every word we exchange.

Darcy handles it with her usual grace, waltzing over to a wall of animals and finding me a ceramic kitten. She gets me set up at my own station, explaining the process of getting the paints and all the layers that are required to make the ceramic look good after it's put in the kiln.

"I'll just be painting it black," I say.

She plops down a whole bottle of black paint she'd already grabbed for me. "I figured. Just keep it at your table. It's easier that way."

Once I begin to work on my kitten, she mills around for longer than I anticipate. Hovering, really. Pam's Paints isn't wide, but it's long. There are a lot of alcoves and clutter, as well as treasures available for purchase, including any number of Fableview-themed ornaments and magnets. Plenty of things for her to adjust. And other people to attend to. But she stays here with me.

In any other circumstance, I would want her around. Smelling her bodywash, coming up with any clever remark I could think of just to see that smile on her face, to know I'm the one who made her laugh.

Right now I need her far away.

"Would you mind giving me some space?" I ask. "I'm not . . . um . . . connected to my muse."

Darcy searches my face for a clue that I'm kidding. The tension that coils around my throat doesn't show in my expression. This is what sitting behind her in French has taught me to do.

"No problem. I'll be up front if you need anything." She's

given me a seat behind the counter. If she faces forward in her chair, I'll be out of her eyeline. But she *doesn't* face forward. She looks back in near-constant intervals. I start counting them out, and it averages every twenty-eight seconds.

It stretches to thirty-five.

Then to over a minute.

My ceramic cat has about three intentional strokes of black paint across its belly and seven random blotches of paint from me losing my focus. "You're still distracting me," I tell her.

"Sorry, sorry!" she says, throwing her hands up in playful surrender. "I would never want to interrupt your muse."

"It's fickle. Delicate."

"Of course." She makes a big show of getting out her phone, tilting her head down to start scrolling through it.

I wait a respectful minute, making sure she's truly lost in the land of apps, before I stand up. It's risky with my back turned to her, but I commit to it, moving in my slow, silent way. I've gotten very good at not pulling focus, slipping between the cracks of other people's lives, like a blur only remembered if caught on the edge of a photo. It's easier than taking up their attention, because once I have it, all they ever seem to care about is what I can do with my powers.

Mere feet from achieving my goal, something stops me in my tracks. It's not a mirage or a figment of my nightmares. It's *Julia*, sitting in Pam's Paints, painting purple stripes onto the socks of a witch figurine. She hasn't looked up from her work in progress, her curly red hair so large and full that it's falling into her face.

I open and close the supply closet door, keeping the handle twisted until the door shuts silently behind me. It's a cramped space, filled to capacity with *things*. Half-finished paintings resting against shelves of unpainted ceramics. A long table pushed up against the side, covered in scrap materials. My heart is beating so hard it hurts.

Julia is here.

She's become so significant in my memories that the reality of her is hard to process. Even when I thought I saw her at the pumpkin patch, her presence felt more like a manifestation of my anxieties than an actual possibility. I've spent years poring over all the things she said to me. I haven't spent any of our time apart considering what *I'd* say to *her*.

In the far corner of the supply closet, there is a wooden table covered in splatters of paint.

Atop it, all three of the ceramics that were broken last week lie in organized pieces with a bottle of super glue beside them. The gnome has been partially reassembled. He is fragmented and sad, missing half of his left eye, all of his nose, and a triangle of one cheek.

Seeing this, knowing what these little pieces mean to Darcy, helps me regain my focus. Julia might be inside Pam's Paints, but she's not in this closet. She can't reach me here. Not yet.

Usually I need to think of something related to my task, like the colors of the paints used or the way the ceramics feel in my hand, glossy and smooth. For this, I find Darcy's face is enough.

I inhale, focusing on the sweet flattery in her expression when we talked about this gnome the first night I came here, then exhale, keeping my hands cupped over the broken gnome.

The magic inside me builds, a pressure I can feel into the roof of my mouth, like a yawn I've swallowed. I imagine the gnome as he once was, picture each broken piece finding its match, and the tension inside my body begins to spill into my hands, re-assembling the gnome.

There's a sense of completion when I succeed. It's the same satisfaction I get when I answer the last question on a test, and I know the work is done.

Opening my eyes, the little gnome greets me, looking the same as he did when we first met.

I scrape up the pieces of the broken mug next, making it into a pile. It's best to have my materials close together so the magic doesn't have to stretch too far to find what I need. I learned that the hard way while training with my cousin Graham. We were working on the distance of my magic, exploring how far my mending could go to repair something. We'd already figured out I could gather materials that weren't in immediate view. That day we wanted to see if I could repair things for which I had no supply, like patching a gap in his roof without having extra shingles.

Graham stood behind me as I squatted down, my hands atop the missing shingle. I focused my breathing. Imagined the ceiling below free of a drip. Envisioned the piece of roof folding over itself to be fixed.

Next thing I knew, Graham was doubled over. I'd conjured a shingle out of thin air, and it had hit him in the head on its way to me. He was inches from falling off the roof altogether.

"That was *awesome*," he'd said, blood trickling down his forehead. "Your power is amazing."

This ceramic mug has most of its pieces, but some are so fine, they are nearly powder. I make the mountain of fragments as contained as possible, and my hand catches on a particularly sharp piece, slicing the skin between my thumb and forefinger.

"Shit," I say, louder than I mean to, startling backward as I put the cut to my mouth to nurse it. There is a wall of ceramics behind me, waiting to be glazed. My abrupt movement makes them wobble in dramatic fashion—loud, sharp clanks that anyone in the shop can hear.

The door handle turns.

# 13

# DARCY

I've always thought our supply closet was small. Now it's *too* small. *Smell the oils on Anya's skin* small. Hear her short, interrupted intake of breath as I readjust myself to approach her. She's all stormy eyes and intense energy, working very hard to back away even when there's nowhere to go.

"What are you doing in here?" I ask.

She has her lips cupped over the inside of her palm. "I cut myself."

My worry overrides my suspicion, and I push forward. "Let me see."

Once my hand is on her wrist, she relents without hesitation. The cut is long, stretching over the delicate skin between her thumb and finger.

"This is a tricky spot," I say. It's hard to focus with that heady, herbal scent that emanates off her body every time we're this close.

I release her hand to move to the other side of the supply

closet, where we keep a small first aid kit. Every movement is a dance, clumsy and urgently close, an unchoreographed tango where one of us needs to take the lead.

"Take a seat," I tell her, letting it be me.

She follows my directions without resistance, settling down in the chair I'd placed in front of the table to work on fixing my ceramics. I'm still not used to the pressure of her attention, the way it makes me so aware of myself, wondering what it is she thinks of my every hand movement and hair flick.

The wound isn't deep, but the paper-thin skin in this part of her hand makes the cut look worse than it is. I have to use up the last of the gauze to staunch the blood flow, wrapping and wrapping until there is no visible red. My work looks excessive, like she's a boxer getting ready for a match, but it's better to be safe than sorry.

"You're very good at taking care of things," she says.

"Someone has to be," I tell her, keeping my eyes on the bandages. "Now, can you explain how you got this?"

"I fell."

"You fell?" I repeat.

"Yes."

The silence swells. Suffocating. Close. I have no choice but to look at her. To lock into my determination to know what's actually happening.

The longer we look at each other, the less I remember what I'm wondering about. Her eyes, keen, focused, are such a crystallized color. Syrup-on-pancakes brown. And her lips have this permanent quirk to them, forever skeptical. I'd like to wipe that expression off her face. I'd like to see who else she could become with me around.

I lean closer, possessed by a need that's greater than all my other senses.

"Do you want to come to a dinner with my parents and me next week?" she blurts out, my mouth inches from hers.

It startles me back into my body, returning my thoughts to my brain instead of whatever distant planet they'd gone to, where I thought I was someone else.

I'm holding both her hands, bandaged and regular. Squeezing them, really. I'm kneeling between her legs.

I almost kissed her.

She repeats the question, which is good, because I've already forgotten it.

"My parents are coming into town next week, and they asked me to bring a *friend* to dinner. If you want to come," she says. She makes a show of emphasizing "friend." Because that's how she sees me.

God.

She's trying to let me down gently.

I fly upright, so embarrassed I can barely contain myself. This supply closet is packed with random things. Every move has dangerous reverberations, shaking paintings and creations.

"I'd love that," I say, forcing myself to be as cheery about this as a friend would. We are definitely friends. I guess? I've never once thought of Anya as that. She's kind of existed in her own world. But it makes sense. She's my friend. Of course she is.

That's great. Perfect.

We can do that.

"Really?" she asks, then she seems to think better of it. "I'll text you more later. But I have to go. Sorry I didn't finish my ceramic." She sticks her unbandaged hand into her pocket and pulls out two twenty-dollar bills. "Here. Let me know if I need to give you more."

My whole world spins. I can't slow it down enough to stop her, still processing the almost kiss, and the dinner invite, and her slipping into the supply closet in the first place. She skirts past me, letting herself out.

I should follow her. Tell her to stay. But I'm frozen in place, confused and overwhelmed. It's good to be in the chaos of this room, like being closed inside my own private disaster cocoon. I slump into the chair she's vacated, needing to catch my breath.

My dad's broken mug has been organized into a tighter pile than I left it in, with a splatter of blood beside it. This is where Anya was standing when I found her. This is what she was doing. I'm so caught up on why she'd want to fix my broken ceramics that I almost miss it. My gnome.

He has no visible cracks. Not a single piece is out of place. If I didn't know better, I'd think he'd never been broken at all. He looks exactly as he did when I first made him, shiny and small and sweet.

But I *know* he was broken. I swept him into a dustpan myself, then spent the last week painstakingly sorting each shard, making piles to begin the tedious process of rebuilding what I'd destroyed. In less than five minutes, Anya seems to have completely fixed him, the same way she fixed Maddie's wings.

I throw open the supply closet door, prepared to chase Anya all the way down Fableview Boulevard. It's time she gives me some *real* answers. There is no getting out of it this time.

I don't have to do that, because she's still here, talking to one of our other customers.

This would be weird enough on its own. I've never even seen

Anya speak to her own aunt. But the look on Anya's face is unlike anything I've ever experienced either. Her skin has turned a bluish white. Her eyes are red and watery. Those lips I wished to paint hang open in a soft *O* shape.

She's talking to someone I don't recognize. She must be one of the tourists here for the full Fableview experience.

I'm weighing my options, deciding how much I want to ask Anya in front of this person. It's like we're back in the supply closet again. She's hurt, and I can't help but insert myself into the situation to fix it.

"Hello," I say brightly, stretching my hand out to greet the other girl. "I know we met when you came in, but I'm Darcy, Anya's friend." The word "friend" still feels like a weapon. At least this time I can repurpose it for a better cause.

"Oh, wow, hi." As the girl shakes my hand, she does a full-body assessment of me. It's quick, not meant to make a point or anything, but I still notice it. "I'm Julia."

*Julia.* The person Anya brought up at the pumpkin patch, who once told Anya that she didn't care about other people's feelings.

"Nice to meet you," I say, giving away nothing. "Do you guys know each other?" I keep all my attention on Julia even as Anya gives me her most intense, focused stare. She wants me to look over, to send me some kind of signal that this is *the girl*. But I know how badly this Julia hurt her in the past. And judging by how upset Anya looked when I emerged from the supply closet, Julia's still hurting her now. Playing ignorant will take away some of Julia's power.

"Anya used to live in my hometown, yeah," Julia says.

"Cool! We love having her in Fableview. Isn't she the best?"

This might be too far, but I've already decided I hate this Julia girl, and I don't mind daring her to speak poorly of Anya to my face. I know for certain Anya's not a bad person. And I also know with proof that she absolutely thinks about other people. She came all the way to the art shop to fix my ceramics, and she didn't even want me to know she'd done it. She might be the most generous person I've ever met.

"This place is great," Julia says, avoiding my question altogether. "I've been staying at the Fableview Inn with my boyfriend. We road-tripped here." She points to the guy she came with, who is still painting his ceramic. He doesn't look up to acknowledge us.

"I love the Fableview Inn," I tell her.

"It's amazing. This whole town is. I'm obsessed with witchy stuff."

"You're certainly in the right place for that."

"I really have to go," Anya blurts out, cutting off this exchange of pleasantries. "Bye, Darcy. Thanks again." She hurries out of the shop, leaving me with Julia and her silent boyfriend.

There is no way I can follow her now. That will let Julia know that Anya and I have something to discuss, and the less Julia knows about anything, the better.

Without Anya around, Julia's whole demeanor changes. The friendly smile she'd had plastered on her face falls. "You know, right? About Anya?"

I hate the way she says this, so full of sneering judgment, as if I'd ever be a member of whatever Anya Doyle hate club she wants to form.

"Of course I do," I say with confidence.

"Okay, good. Just be careful, then," she warns. "She'll lie

straight to your face, over and over, and she won't feel bad about it."

I give her a tight smile. "Got it. Let me know if you need any help with the ceramics."

"Okay, thanks." She sits back down, dabbing off the fine-tipped brush she'd been using to do stripes on her witch figurine's socks.

The thing is, Anya *does* lie. She lied to me just now, in the supply closet. She lied that first night she came here to the shop, and again when she fixed Maddie's wings. I want to know why she's done all that, why she never seems to tell me anything fully honest, but the last person I want to learn that information from is Julia.

I'm halfway to the front desk when Julia blurts out my name. I turn back, and she's looking at me pleadingly as she says, "Whatever you do, don't trust her."

# 11 Days Until Halloween

# 14

# ANYA

It's bad when even the sad girl music doesn't cut it for me. Sometimes it's too on the nose, and what I really need to listen to are the brightest, happiest songs I can find. Not because I dislike this kind of music. It's that, when I'm really in my feelings, joy seems like the saddest emotion of all.

I have my headphones on, upbeat pop blaring loud enough to make me lose hearing as I do French extra credit to keep my mind occupied. A loud sound from outside cuts in just enough to make me pause.

It's a car. Honking. Not once, not twice, but *six* times in urgent succession. Aunt Cal's sitting room has giant curtains that are always closed. They're made of a heavy red fabric that might be as old as the house itself. I tug one back a fraction of an inch, holding my breath to avoid inhaling whatever volatile combination of dust and filth I've just kicked up.

There's a black SUV parked in front of Cal's house. The driver honks again, and it's a siren song to my nervous system. All these years of hearing my family talk about threats to our magic—years of me tuning it out, thinking it's some kind of vague thing they've made up to make us all feel self-important—now seems like the greatest oversight of my life.

Julia is here, and she has come to make a spectacle of the way I once failed her.

Or worse, she's told Darcy everything, and Darcy herself is here to force answers out of me about why, when she moved so close to me, angling to have our lips meet, I *invited her to a family dinner* instead. The very dinner I'd already decided would never, under any circumstance, actually happen.

I'll have to fight this attack with nothing but my French vocabulary and my heaviest glare. Lucky for me, the glare is surprisingly effective, according to multiple outside sources.

The honking continues—a long, persistent blare interrupted by occasional short beeps. I surrender to my fate, opening Cal's front door a sliver.

*Let me surrender in peace. No need to involve the entire street.*

My head is no more than six inches out into the open when I hear "There she is!"

Pulling the door open all the way, I see . . . my mother?

Yes. My mother. Is here. Right now. Six days ahead of her already-early plan to show up.

"Goodness, you've gotten taller," she says. "I hope Cal's been measuring! It's at least two inches!" She has her hand over her forehead to gaze up at me, standing beside the SUV—her SUV, I recognize now—as my dad ambles his way around to the trunk.

"Hello," he says with a quick wave, greeting me more like a neighbor than a father. I appreciate his subdued reaction, because my body refuses to move any farther even as my brain tells me to run into the woods and take refuge. It's one thing to lie to my parents over the phone. Not easy, but manageable. In person, my mom's brightness is so overwhelming that I can't help but wither like the aster I burned on Fableview Boulevard.

I knew this moment would come, but I hoped I'd be more ready. I wanted to have a set plan for my nonwitch life.

"When we talked to you the other day and saw how beautiful the town looked, we just couldn't help ourselves! We went ahead and moved our flight up again," Mom explains as Dad hauls two massive pink suitcases out of the trunk. "One has clothes for me to wear. The other's full of clothes I need you to fix! My little mender!"

My dad reaches into the trunk again, taking out what must be his bag—a small leather backpack that he slings across his right shoulder, likely holding the three repeats of the same dark brown sweater he has on now. Feeling the tiniest bit of mercy for him, I walk down the stairs to help carry Mom's giant bags inside.

He gives me a quick squeeze. "I wanted to tell you, but she insisted it be a surprise."

"It's definitely a surprise," I reply.

Mom reaches for me from behind. I turn to meet her, and she holds me so tight to her chest that what remains of my breath gets lost in the fabric of her shirt—a loud, floral blouse with dangling flower earrings to match. She starts kissing my head in comical fashion. Aggressive smooches of joy that I find embarrassing even when our only audience is Dad, who is used to it by now.

Done with her squishing, Mom takes me by the shoulders and scans me. "I need to see you up close."

When we look at each other eye to eye, I feel as though I can imagine all the different people we've been before. One of the witches in our family has the gift of viewing past lives. She's told me more than once that my mother was once my child. It's strange to feel that now, to see in my mom's eyes that she's more innocent than I am. She trusts the world in a way I do not, sees the beauty in making friends and having community. Between us, she's the one with hope for life. I'm the bitter cynic who knows better.

For an amazing moment, all my worries melt away, replaced by sentimental adoration.

*My mom is here.*

Then I remember that this is exactly what I will be giving up when I leave our coven. My escape, my attempt at a normal life, will come at the cost of my family. There will be no sentimental hugs after long periods of being apart. No wet kisses on my forehead and overbearing questions about my inner life.

I will belong to no one.

Aunt Cal walks around from the back of her winding Victorian home wearing her patchwork jacket and a large straw sun hat. She's carrying a basket of radishes she's picked from the garden.

"Cal!" Mom yells. "You look radiant as ever!"

Aunt Cal makes no change to her expression. She puts down her basket of radishes and stands still, waiting for my mom to give her the inevitable smothering hug we all know is coming.

My mom meets the moment in the exact way we anticipated. "My baby sister," she coos, clobbering Cal. "As beautiful as always."

Cal finally gives in and hugs my mom back. It really is

impossible to remain passive around a woman as vibrant as Mom. She's so potent, and yet she's surrounded by stoic types like Dad, Aunt Cal, and me. She's the one who makes us all softer.

Cal goes stiff, and immediately my mom releases her, knowing what this means—Cal's having a vision.

Her body stays rigid, and she gets a far-off look in her eyes, like she's been transported to whatever it is she's seeing. It's the kind of thing Darcy would never believe is real. She'd say that Cal is just doing a bit of visual theater before suggesting things that are already likely to happen, and through that, it makes them come true. But Cal has predicted things no one could ever know in advance. She's prevented car accidents that occurred with other drivers in the same intersection she named. She's seen pregnancies even the mothers didn't yet know about. Her powers may not be as tangible as mine, but they are definitely real.

This particular vision lasts about three seconds. Cal stands taut—eyes vacant, hands fixed into fists—as Mom, Dad, and I wait to hear what she's seen. What a sight we must make to the neighbors. This is the kind of strange that only makes sense in a place like Fableview.

When it's done, Cal relaxes back to her usual self.

"You aren't being truthful," she says, looking right at me. Her first words spoken in almost two months.

I fumble for a response. Defensive. Confused. Amused. None of it seems right.

I choose to say, "How so?" needing more than anything to know exactly what it is that she's seen. I'm not being truthful about a lot of things. Which is the one she's found worth mentioning? And what will happen because of it?

Does she know what my life will look like without our coven? Could she give me a hint?

With a glint in her eye, she says, *"Not now,"* and ushers my parents inside.

My mom and dad are unbothered by this foreboding message. My mom has known Cal her whole life. And my dad makes it a point not to be bothered by much of anything. Neither of them even casts a sideways glance my way. They walk inside—Mom with an excited smile, Dad with his usual calm expression—both of them commenting on how nice the place looks since the last time they visited.

In reality, Cal's house is a labyrinth of old books and half-melted candles piled indiscriminately in different corners, with those giant velvet curtains blocking out most of the sunlight. It's best in here on a rainy day, when the cloudless sky turns everything stark and Cal lights a fire for us to gather around.

Today, with the sun shining brightly through the autumn-turned leaves, my parents in town and Cal aware of my lies, the house feels suffocating. Too full of a history I can't live up to and a past that's overdue to catch me. This would be the time for me to come clean. But I can't do it. I'd rather suffer the consequences all at once than drag it out over the next two weeks.

Once my parents have brought their luggage to their guest room and caught up with Cal about various family topics, Mom claps her hands together and says, "So! When do we get to meet the famous Darcy?"

All day I have been working to avoid the thought of her. When Julia stopped me in Pam's Paints, the first thing she had to say to me, after all these years, was "Of course you'd be here. Who are you going after this time?"

As if she weren't the one who'd targeted *me*. Sought me out, knowing I came from a family of witches. *She* made me her friend. *She* used me.

It's taken me years to accept that. I've been so caught up in the mean things she said to me, trying desperately to fix it, that I haven't allowed myself to admit that I didn't deserve any of it in the first place.

I made the right choice by not helping her with my powers.

But she's here at the worst possible time. A time when Darcy almost kissed me. It's the kind of hopeless utopia that would swallow me whole, until one day I got regurgitated back into the real world—where Darcy Keller is a girl from Fableview who's destined to go somewhere else, and I am a girl from somewhere else who's destined to go nowhere.

"Darcy's busy," I tell my mom. Another truth. Darcy somehow teaches art classes, runs the art club, sings in the school choir, helps her parents organize the Halloween schedule, *and* attends every event. In a themed costume, no less. She is the definition of "busy."

Cal, with a knowing smile, revealing more with her face than she has with her words, says, "We should go see her at the apple orchard."

"Yes! I *love* the apple orchard," my mom says.

It's not fair. My mom loves most things.

"I don't think so," I say. "She has a lot on her plate. We should get food instead. I'm sure my parents are hungry."

Maybe this is what Cal saw—me being dishonest with myself. The most beautiful girl I've ever seen was seconds away from kissing me, and I stopped her in the worst way possible, by inviting her to a dinner that was never supposed to happen. A dinner that will now get moved up the moment Darcy sees my parents are here ahead of schedule.

"Embarrassing" doesn't even begin to cover it.

"We should go to the apple orchard," Cal repeats.

"I liked you better when you'd taken a vow of silence," I say.

# 15

## DARCY

"No costume?" Grace asks, pointing to my overalls. She doesn't bother with shielding her horror. It's almost funny with prosthetics glued to her cheeks and a light green body paint covering her skin. I'm being judged by an alien for dressing normally.

"It wasn't meant to be a statement," I say. But maybe it was. I wanted to look cute just to be cute, not look cute as a character.

Everything has felt different since the almost kiss. I couldn't muster up the interest in putting on my costume and pretending to be something I'm not, because it seems like I'm pretending everywhere in life, and putting on one more costume would be a bridge too far.

"You're being very mysterious these days," Grace says, waving her green fingers in my face.

Piper walks up with a crate of apples. She's wearing one of her hand-embroidered sweaters. This one has a single tiny apple in the left corner. No one gives her a hard time about her mild commitment to our event themes. Not that I think we should start. Splitting time between her divorced parents' houses is already tough enough on her. I'm just feeling the weight of my own burdens in a way I haven't before. The pressure to be perfect all season long.

"Will Anya be joining us?" Piper asks, never one for subtlety.

"I'm sure she'll skip this," I tell them both.

"I'm sure she won't," Grace says, more to Piper than me. The two of them laugh. Then Grace picks up an apple from the crate and takes a bite. "You know, she's not as sinister as I first thought."

Grace's opinions of people tend to be stubbornly fixed. Even if someone has spent years proving her otherwise, she almost always goes back to her gut.

"She's definitely not sinister," I confirm, wanting to validate this. If nothing else, I would like my friends to like Anya. Since Anya is apparently *also* my friend. A friend with secrets. A friend who Julia told me not to trust. Not that Julia's worth trusting herself. But something specific happened between them that I don't know about, and it seems connected to everything else I don't know about Anya.

"You're right. Anya's kind of, like . . ." Grace lets the thought hang, searching for a word that's very obvious to me.

"Thoughtful," I fill in for her.

"Exactly," Grace says. "And she's also, like . . . I don't know . . . kind of . . ." She waves her half-bitten apple around.

"Funny?" I guess. Grace doesn't accept that one, so I keep going. "Observant?"

"Amazing?" Piper interjects. "Incredible? Perfect in every way?"

She and Grace exchange a smirking look.

Whenever Piper's out of town, Grace is only at half strength. And while Grace and I have always been the true best friend duo, Piper strengthens us both. We need a third party who can split the difference when we're stuck, and Piper settles well into that role. Really she fits into any role. She's a chameleon in that way, flitting in and out of all the Fableview High friend groups with ease. She's only a junior, and I forget it constantly, because she's that good at slipping into the middle of any moment and acting like she's been there the entire time, when she's usually around for only half of it.

This was a setup, and I fell right into the trap.

"We need to get these over to my parents," I say, lifting the crate Piper just set down and walking away with it. While it's inconvenient to carry thirty pounds of apples that are already exactly where they need to be, it's the kind of grueling task I welcome. "More apples are here," I tell my mom.

She's busy chatting up the mayor. She casts one quick look my way and then another, longer double take, her mortification only thinly disguised by her Frankenstein's bride makeup. "Did something happen to your costume?" she asks, employing the same hushed urgency she'd use if I walked out of the bathroom with toilet paper on my shoe.

"I decided to dress in the spirit of the event instead," I tell her. "Apple bobbing feels very overalls and pigtail braids to me."

"You've *really* made it your mission to do things differently this year," she comments.

It's the first clue she's even been paying attention to any of my subtle tweaks this season.

"Change is good," I say. "For my new era as owner."

We stare at each other.

"Does this have anything to do with your friend?" Dad interjects. "The one who joined the committee?"

"She's not my friend," I say defensively, still prickly from Grace and Piper's attempts to approach me on the subject. "I mean, yes, she is. But it's nothing to do with that."

But really, Anya isn't my friend. Or she isn't *just* my friend. She is not like Grace or Piper. She's not like Kyle Holtzenberg. She's her own category. A hands-shaking, palms-sweating category that I'm still in the process of developing.

Dad puts his hands up. He didn't intend to provoke me, unlike Grace and Piper. "No worries. I just want you to know you can always talk to me."

"Thanks," I tell him. It's amusing how much he means it. There's sincerity in his eyes, and I feel it in the way he hugs me close, all fatherly sentimentality, surely thinking something like *My baby girl is growing up.* But when I do something as mild as wear overalls to the apple picking contest instead of dressing up in a costume, it's a cause of conflict. He hasn't given me any room to actually confide in him.

"Do you want me to put these apples back where they belong?" Mom asks.

"Oh, sorry, I thought maybe you guys needed some."

"Last I checked, all the apples we need will be baked into the pies we're judging," she says, more to the mayor, who has been standing a few feet away, obviously listening to the three of us. *The families of Fableview, building the texture of our quaint little town.* "But maybe you should take a break from your friends and help us out with the pie contest. We haven't gotten to enjoy many activities together this year."

Normally this would be an uninteresting idea. More time with my parents sounds like a recipe for stress. Right now, having a reason to do things without Grace and Anya to pester me sounds ideal. "Yeah, that works."

When I carry the apple crate back to Grace and Piper, I pretend it was my parents' error.

"They thought they might need some, but they realized that if they do, they'll just come get them from you guys," I say, dropping it off and heading back in the direction of the pies.

"You're not hosting the bobbing contest with me?" Grace calls out. She's spoken it through her handheld voice modulator. Still, the hurt in her voice is clear, even with warbles in it intended to make her sound like she's not of this Earth.

"My parents want me to spend time with them. And I've been doing so much rule breaking behind their backs that it's probably a good idea to hang out with them. Renew their goodwill," I say.

Grace starts up a conversation with Piper, no modulator involved. It's the kind intended for me to overhear—loud, with overly emphasized syllables—but I tune it out, not needing any more judgment.

I will enjoy this event in peace. Eat some good pies and share some laughs with my parents. Next year their life will be my life. I might as well find some new things to love about it.

Working the contest turns out to be genuinely fun. The entries are amazing. There are apple pies done up in every way possible, from classic cinnamon and sugar to more adventurous offerings, like a maple bacon Gruyère that is surprisingly delightful.

I'm midway through my third bite of a salted caramel entry—my contender for first place—when Mom says through a mouthful of her own serving, "Oh, look. There's your friend."

To my horror, she's pointing.

At Anya.

Anya walks—sulks, more accurately—beside her Aunt Cal. There are two more people next to them. A man with a brooding mysteriousness that matches Anya's, and a smiling older woman dressed in bright florals, waving at every person they pass. These must be Anya's parents. Somehow, they seem like two sides of her coin. The dad obviously captures her dark, moody exterior. But beneath that is a secret, gooey softness that matches her mom's. When Anya invited me to dinner with them, I swore she said they were coming next week.

Yet here they are right now, with my mom pointing at them, practically beckoning them forward.

# 16

# ANYA

My mom and the Kellers have spotted each other, and I still don't have a plan.

I need an escape, and fast.

Searching for an answer, my eyes land on Grace. She's dressed as an alien, but that's no longer an oddity. It's weirder now when I see her in school. She looks incomplete without a fully committed costume.

"Hey!" I say, running over to join her before I can consider what it means. I need to buy at least three minutes away from my mom before I'm forced to admit that the whole thing about being friends with Darcy is a lie. Or before I admit something even worse, like my plan to leave the coven altogether.

Grace arches one eyebrow as she asks, "You want to bob for apples?"

"No," I say, trying out a friendly laugh, attempting to encourage her penchant for long-winded speeches.

"Then why are you up here?"

My terror dawns fast and burns bright. In reaching Grace, I have walked myself right into the apple bobbing contest. There are three contestants standing farther down the stage. They each have a giant bucket of apple-filled water atop a long table in front of them. There is one more open bucket with no one waiting behind it.

"Actually"—my throat is so dry that I have to clear it two times before I can finish my sentence—"I *do* want to bob for apples."

"Really?" Grace doesn't bother to hide her skepticism, which she has every right to have.

My head fights my attempt to nod. *"Mm-hmm."* No part of me wants to bob for apples in front of Fableview locals and tourists alike, but what am I going to do, run back down the stairs? Rejoin my family in their quest to find Darcy? Admit everything in front of the entire town?

Grace leans toward my ear. "Darcy's not here," she whispers. "She didn't want to help me with this for some reason." She says it both sympathetically and accusatorily, like it might be a disappointment to me but is somehow also my fault. Either way, she thinks Darcy is the reason I've decided to apple bob in the first place.

She is, but not in the way Grace thinks. If this is a place where Darcy isn't, then this is the exact place I want to be. And it's where I want my family to be too.

"No worries," I say. I chance a glance into the audience and see my parents and Cal have stopped to watch this, all three of them equally confused by my unexpected interest in apple bobbing.

So far, this is working out as well as it could have.

Grace hands me a pair of lime-green goggles, and it's no

longer working out as great as possible, but it's still better than the alternative. I swallow back my rising dread as I take the last spot in the lineup, next to who else but Kyle Holtzenberg. At least my participation now has some interest beyond avoiding my family's search for Darcy Keller. I may not be good at many things, but I am good at beating other people when it counts. And I'd love to beat Kyle Holtzenberg at this.

"You *would* do this," I say to him.

"What's your deal?" Kyle asks. "You don't speak a single word to anyone all year, and then suddenly you're everywhere I am. Tell me honestly. Are you, like, in love with me?"

My face muscles almost twitch. The laugh is right there, desperate to escape, but I push it down. "Finally, you've noticed," I deadpan. "It's been impossible to keep it in. I came up here to spell out 'I love you' in apples, but this works too."

Kyle looks to our other competitors for sympathy. I don't recognize either of them. One of them is wearing a shirt from Witches of Fableview. A tourist, most likely.

"I really can't tell if you're joking." There's a plain urgency in his voice that makes me want to soften a bit. It's not very fun to play these kinds of games when the other party doesn't understand the rules.

"I'm not in love with *you*," I say, putting an unintended emphasis on the word "you." It comes out sounding like I'm in love with someone else.

Kyle gives me a pesky scowl, like he knows exactly who it is. I scowl back. The both of us are ten seconds away from sticking our heads into buckets of apples and slobbering around until we can gather a bunch of them into other buckets. No one knows anything up here, about any of this.

"There will be one minute on the clock," Grace announces. "The person to successfully drop the most apples from their bucket into the container at their feet is the winner."

"What's the prize?" I ask.

Kyle scoffs. "You don't even know what you're doing this for?"

"I'm doing this for you, baby." Forget taking it easy on him. I need to take it harder. The competition has already begun.

Grace relishes the chance to show me the prize, reaching behind her podium to hoist up a giant trophy with an apple at the top of it. "This is only for the grand prize winner, though," she cautions. "You're in the first of five semifinals right now."

"You get five hundred dollars if you win it all," Kyle whispers. "So I'd appreciate it if you didn't mess up my flow. I want that money."

"So do I," I say.

I *need* it, actually, for when I turn down the chance to join my family's coven and begin my regular life.

Piper comes around to tie my hands together with a bandana. "Do you want me to go tell Darcy you're competing?"

I pull the green goggles over my eyes. They provide me enough privacy to really let her question roll off my back. "That's not necessary," I say.

"Well, I think you guys are cute together," she tells me. "And I have a gift for knowing this sort of stuff."

Both of Darcy's closest friends have now mentioned her to me, and Piper's made it sound like we're *something*. What has Darcy told them? And what else does Piper know? She has that same energy about her that Grace does—that knowing. The only person I've ever been fooling about anything might really be Darcy.

Piper ties up my hands.

Grace begins the countdown.

There is a brief moment when I entertain the ridiculousness of this—me, Anya Doyle, in an apple bobbing contest. Then Grace calls out, "Go," and I plunge my face into the bucket, and the water is so cold and the apples are so slippery that all my self-consciousness disappears. It feels the same as my magic, the way my breath steadies my body, all my focus and intention going toward my singular goal. Grab every apple I can.

My teeth find something to hold, and I bite down, then spit out the apple into the basin at my feet. It's exhilarating. Fun, even. There is no sense of time and place, only me and this task.

Dive. Bite. Plop.

Dive. Bite. Plop.

When it's done, Grace calls out time, thrusting me back into the now. I'm drenched from head to toe, water splashed down my shirt and onto my jeans and boots and in a pool three feet wide around my body. My short hair is stuck to my forehead and cheeks, sopping wet and cold.

Piper unties the bandana around my wrists. "That was incredible," she says.

Heaving, I pull the goggles off my face and look over at Kyle's bucket. He's done very well. It will be close.

I look out into the audience, prepared to see my family's amused faces. This will be a nice last memory of me they can cherish after I'm forced to move to god knows where and fend for myself.

But it's Darcy I see instead. Front row.

# 17

# DARCY

Grace taps the mic to gain everyone's attention. "The winner of our first-round semifinal, with an amazing twenty-six apples captured in a minute, is Anya Doyle!"

Anya sulks her way to the front, claiming the smaller semi-final trophy.

"We'll have four more semifinal rounds, so it's not too late to enter," Grace announces afterward.

Kyle jumps off the front of the stage, making a beeline for me. "Can you tell your girlfriend to leave me alone?" he asks. "She sabotaged me up there, cutting in front of this old guy who was just about to volunteer to be the fourth bobber. Did you put her up to it? I just—"

He's still talking, but my mind has snagged on "girlfriend." He called Anya my girlfriend. And it wasn't even judgmental. At least not judgmental of us dating. Judgmental only of Anya beating him. Why does Kyle think that? And why did Anya do the apple bobbing contest in the first place?

"I have to go," I tell him, cutting off whatever point he's rambling on about. "If you're nice enough, I'm sure Grace will let you enter another semifinal." Grace would never break the rules like that, but it's the only way to get Kyle off my trail. He can't be stalking behind me, distressed about his loss, when I have more important things to handle.

Anya slinks off the stage with her trophy and the towel Grace has handed her. She's out of view from the rest of the audience, hiding between the back curtain of the stage and the side of a tent. There are stray props back here. Extra medals and ribbons. Tubs full of unused decorations.

I'm not sure what energy I have, but I have a lot of it, and it has me storm up to Anya and say her name like an accusation. She startles, fumbling the towel she'd been cupping around the ends of her hair.

The wobbly, heart-squeezing feeling inside me only swells at the sight of her this close. There are goggle indents around her eyes and a red oval on either side of her nose. Her black tank top is wet, with her black cardigan falling off her shoulder. Her chin-length hair is usually stick straight and tucked behind her ears. Now it's flung across her face, stuck to her cheeks.

For whatever reason, despite all of it, the first thing that comes to my mind is, "Is your hand okay?"

Forget the gnome, Maddie's wings, Julia's comment, the family dinner invite, Anya's participation in the apple bobbing contest. I need to know that she didn't get too hurt in the shop.

Anya looks down at the new bandage she's put there, much smaller than the one I placed on her. It's one of the only dry things on her body after the bobbing, thanks to her hands being tied behind her back.

"It's totally fine," she tells me.

"That's good," I say. I have an instinct to reach for her, examine it like a doctor at a follow-up appointment, to make sure this isn't yet another thing she's been lying to me about. "You're into apples?"

"Oh yeah. Big time," she says back, letting a tiny sliver of a smile creep onto her face.

My stomach does an unexpected flip, setting me off-kilter. "Congrats on your win up there."

"Someone had to put Kyle Holtzenberg in his place."

"He's *so* offended you won. I barely escaped his complaining. He told me to tell my girlfriend to leave him alone."

I watch to see the way the word affects Anya. She'd called me her friend, like a warning or a suggestion I needed to take. But there's a spark that lights up her face when I say "girlfriend" in relation to her. Her hands reach for her heart, her towel clutched against her chest as she takes a moment to look down.

I try to imagine what it's like inside her head, behind the storm cloud of flawless French and silent stewing. If she's back in the supply closet like I am, so close to each other. Living in that *almost*.

"What were you doing with my ceramics?" I ask.

"I was trying to fix everything before it's too late," she says.

"Too late for what?"

"For me. For all of it."

"The gnome looked good as new," I say.

"I was pretty happy with him," she admits. "But I didn't get a chance to finish the rest. Darcy, I—"

"You forgot something else too," I interrupt, stepping closer, no longer capable of ignoring this anymore. Needing, for once, to not have her worried about all the things in my life she wants to help me solve. That's usually my job, finding solutions for other people. Between the two of us, we have a problem that we *both* need to figure out.

"What?" she asks, a flash of worry darting across her face as I close in on her.

"You forgot to kiss me," I say.

Her eyes dart to my lips, then back to my eyes. She drops her towel, and it lands on my feet. I don't sever the delicate tension we've built. If she turns me down, she has to do it to my face. And it's a good thing I keep my eyes on her, because the switch happens in front of me—her expression going from nervous to curious.

"Do you . . . really want me to do that?" she asks, her bottom lip quivering.

"Do you not?"

"I—" She reaches for her towel on the ground, lifting it and then dropping it all over again. "What am I doing? Of course I do." I expect her to wrap me up, the tension snapping like a branch, giving in to something chaotic and urgent.

But this is Anya. She's never what I expect.

She steps on the towel to get her leg between mine. She cups my chin in her hand as she watches me the same way she always does. Like she can see through me, to the core of my being.

"You have no idea who you are to me," she whispers. "How much I don't want to mess this up."

"I don't want to either," I whisper back. There is so much that could complicate this—her secrets, my secrets, everything in between. But when we're this close, none of that seems important.

Her eyes close, long dark lashes fanning gently across her upper cheek as she leans forward. "Are you ready?"

I close my eyes and meet her there, pressing onto my tiptoes to reach her lips for a kiss.

It's so gentle, the same way my heart feels, soft and exploring, like cracking the spine of a book and reading the first page.

Where will this take me? Where can we go?

My hand reaches for the dampness of her back, holding her water-soaked sweater, letting my fist swirl the fabric into a tiny tornado. We're so close that the water's started to soak me too, seeping into my overalls.

"Darcy," she whispers.

I almost open my eyes to look up, but then she kisses me deeper, all the gentle exploration shifting to something bolder. There's a fire in her hands, on her mouth, lighting me up inside. I move my lips to her neck, inhaling the scent of her.

"Anya," I say back, like that's the answer.

Because it is. It feels like this entire month has been a test, a pop quiz about me, and now, with my mouth on Anya's neck and my hands wrapped in her hair, I'm finding the correct answers.

This is who I am.

This is what I want.

And all of it is exactly right.

# 18

## ANYA

I've never snuck out of any house. Not when it's been only Aunt Cal and me, not with any other family member I've stayed with, and certainly not during summer visits with my parents. There has never been a reason for me to leave. Until Darcy. I need to see her again. And I need it, for once, not to be in some setting with every single resident of Fableview around us.

It's easier than I expect, with everyone in their respective bedrooms on the second floor and me above them in the attic, pattering down the back spiral staircase that skips their floor altogether. Even if they did hear me, they'd never suspect this is what I'd be doing.

I drive Aunt Cal's Volkswagen over to Darcy's, pulling into the alley behind Pam's Paints like she instructed. It's a land of dumpsters and unlabeled metal back doors—a nice reminder that even though this town is sometimes unbelievably whole-some, it's also real.

Darcy's bedroom has its own balcony that overlooks the

alley. She swings her leg over the side to find her footing on a pipe. She has a hood pulled over her hair, but her legs are bare, moisturized with something shimmery that catches a glint of moonlight. It's nerve-racking to watch her find a way to the ground, but she has that confidence I know now to be a piece of her. Maybe she's snuck out a dozen times before, and this delicate dance she's doing among pipes and windows and siding is nothing new. Or she knows what we're doing is dangerous but necessary, precious but risky, and one wrong move will mean we can't see each other at all.

"You were right. I do find this car very funny," she tells me as she climbs into Aunt Cal's yellow Beetle. Darcy pulls the hood off her head, revealing the same pigtail braids she had on earlier, now sleep-tousled. She takes in the car's interior. Aunt Cal's drying herbs. All the crystals and talismans Cal's fixed to the dashboard and roped around the rearview mirror.

"It smells like you in here." Darcy presses her nose to my neck.

My foot loses its place on the brake. We wheel forward, and we both shriek.

"I thought you had it in park," Darcy says, sitting very straight now in the passenger seat.

"I wish I did." What a shame that one small decision has resulted in Darcy's distance. The feeling of her nose on my neck still lingers, tickling my skin.

She directs me to Fableview Creek, taking care to keep her hands tucked under her legs for the rest of the drive. I grip the steering wheel tighter, all determination. "Oh," I say. "I won the apple bobbing final."

"I knew you would," she tells me, and my face burns with

pride. "I wish I'd been able to see it, but I was too busy announcing the pie contest winners with my parents."

"A worthy cause."

"Tell me, whatever will you do with your five-hundred-dollar prize?"

"Start a new life."

She laughs like I'm kidding, which is fine. It's better not to complicate this with the specifics anyway.

At the creek, the night is so dark, it blankets everything but the stars, which are countless out here in the stillness. The rush of the river in the near distance roars on with the same intensity as my beating heart—loud and steady. Assured.

"It's really just us out here," I say, parking the car.

"Us and the moon and the animals," Darcy tells me.

"Do you want to sit on the car for a better view?"

Darcy nods, and I pop the trunk to set out one of the large blankets Cal keeps in the back—a patchwork quilt not unlike her signature jacket. It takes some situating, the sloping hood of the Volkswagen not very interested in accommodating us, but eventually we make it work, with the windshield acting as our headboard.

"Thanks for inviting me," Darcy says once we've gotten settled.

And even though we've kissed and I know now that she must like me, it still feels rare to hear her gratitude. *I'd go with you anywhere*, I think but do not say. *You're the best part of every room I'm in.*

We're not touching. Not yet. Close, only inches between us, but not making contact.

"I needed a chance to see you again without the threat of my parents hovering," I say.

"As you know, I can relate," she responds with a small laugh.

It's true. We're both stuck inside our families' expectations. She's got the pressure of being asked to take over her parents' whole empire, which, now that I've had the chance to see it up close, is more work than I'd want to do in a single lifetime.

I've got my family's belief that I'll be participating in the upcoming initiation. I have my eighteenth birthday. Adulthood, supposedly. With no tools to navigate it.

"Mine came to town earlier than I expected," I say. "And before they got here, they asked me to do a dinner with my friends in Fableview, so I may have mentioned your name. Which is why I asked you that. In the supply closet."

This is when I need to convince Darcy I really am a witch. There's no way it won't come up at the actual dinner, and it will be better for all of us if Darcy knows ahead of time.

But just the mention of the supply closet has made everything sharper, like a lens that's locked its focus. Darcy sits up, leaning on her support arm so that she can tuck her head into her own shoulder.

"Are we *friends*?" she asks teasingly, scrunching her nose and singing the words. She plants a quick kiss on my nose. "My dear *friend* Anya." She plants another on my cheek. "Dear, dear *friend*." One on my neck. One on my forehead.

Far be it from me to interrupt these kisses with my inconvenient truth.

"*Mom, Dad, this is Darcy. We're besties,*" I say, catching on to the game. When she darts to kiss me again, I grab her, wrapping my arms around her middle until she's pressed into my chest.

With only one movement, the lack of space between us sucks all the laughter out of the air.

Darcy Keller is on top of me.

I am holding her, feeling her heart against my own, her legs slotting perfectly between mine. It has the odd effect of calming me. Subduing the nerves that want to take hold of this moment.

"I've never dated anyone before," I whisper as low as possible, a secret for Darcy and the stars. "I don't know if I'm doing any of this right."

Her head tilts to the side. It's the same way she looked at the paintings that night I took her class. Curious. Interested. And maybe even a bit . . . admiring? Finally, she drops her head beside mine, presses her lips right against my ear, and whispers, "Are we *dating*?"

It might have been a ridiculous leap to make. But also, every activity we've done around Fableview has felt a little date-like. And, well, she *is* currently on top of me, and all the other pressing matters between us don't seem to matter half as much as this does.

She's got that same teasing tone, but her question is valid. And true. Maybe it's bad form to wonder, but I want to know what we are. There is so much about my life I don't know, but this is something I need to understand.

"I've spent my whole life getting good at change," I say. "I've lived in so many places, adjusting to a dozen different daily routines and rituals. It's always been about how I can fit into someone else's life. How I can learn whatever they want to teach me about our family. I've never had anything that belongs only to me. Except for this, with us. It's mine. *Ours*, really."

"Ours," Darcy echoes. "I like the sound of that." She holds my cheek with her palm, using the pads of her fingers to lightly brush the hair off my face. It's so small. But also, it's everything.

"I don't know exactly what we are, but I know it's something I want to keep figuring out." She strokes my hair.

"Me too," I say.

She kisses me deeply. Slowly. It's a new kind of kiss for us. All of this is new. But this one has a way of speaking. *Whatever we are is the best thing anyone could ever be.*

When she peels herself off me, I don't even mind it. There is no rush. No expectations. She puts her hands behind her head. A drive-in movie theater where the only view is the water.

She pulls one knee up while the other stays flat. I put my finger on it to trace stars into her leg, hypnotized by the softness of her skin and the stillness of the night. How everything just *is*.

I feel the truth about tomorrow's dinner forming in my mind, all the necessary pieces of information gathering together like the supplies that come to me when I'm mending. It might look broken on the surface, but I believe that I can fix it.

"Did you know my grandma was best friends with your grandma?" I start.

"Really?"

"Yeah. According to my mom. Your last name caught her interest."

"Ah, so you mean my dad's mom. I never got to meet either of my grandmas," Darcy tells me. "They both died before I was born. But I feel them a lot. Hard not to, since I'm living in the town they both grew up in, working at the shop one of them owned." She pauses. "Sorry. I don't mean to make it sound like I'm annoyed by my family history. Obviously I'm not. Everyone always says my grandmas were wonderful. I'm not surprised your grandma was best friends with one of them. There's just so much happening right now."

The possibility of her defensiveness won't scare me off. Not this time. Not when I know it's just that—a shield, designed to keep me from seeing her. "How do you do it all?"

"You should be the last person to ask me that," she says. "You must be on track to be our class valedictorian."

Okay, perhaps I'm *not* prepared, because this is not the argument I expected her to make. It derails my entire plan for this reveal. My silence isn't intentional, but she reads it as modesty, and it gets her to slap my arm in that playful way of hers. Then she rests her head in the crook of my shoulder, and I'm happy to be confused if it means having her this close to me again.

"C'mon," she says. "You have a 107 percent in French."

"Because French is the only class you and I have together," I tell her.

She tilts her head, looking at the side of my face with her nose almost pressed into my cheek. I can see the mental math she's doing to accommodate for this admission.

"You're only good at French because you want to beat me at it?" she asks. "You really are competitive. No wonder Kyle fears you."

"I'm good at French because paying attention in that class is the only thing that's kept me from thinking about you the whole time."

It's another heavy thing. Maybe a mistake. But Darcy laughs her real laugh, the one that sounds like wind chimes in a summer breeze. "I'm glad to know I motivate you."

"Oh yes. If you were in all my classes, I probably *would* be valedictorian. But since you're not, I've got B's in everything else. Actually, I almost failed gym class last semester. You can ask Kyle about it. I'm sure he'd love to tell you."

"I will never forget the look on his face when you won the apple bobbing contest," she says.

"Me neither."

We fall quiet. It's on the tip of my tongue. But bringing up the truth will disrupt this perfect peace. I have to hold on to this as long as I can. Because soon I'll have nothing to hold on to at all.

Darcy slides off the top of the car. She opens the passenger door and rummages around for something inside. When she comes back, she has her phone in her hand.

"I want to take a picture," she whispers. I expect to see her align her phone with the water. It would be dark, but maybe she wants it for her art. Something to paint.

Instead she turns the phone toward us, resting her head in the crook of my neck again. "Smile."

I do. How could I not? Because this perfect, fleeting night will exist long beyond my memory of it. No matter who we someday become—Darcy hopefully off to some college far away, me living off five hundred dollars of apple bobbing money somewhere else—there will always be proof of our night by the creek, when the only thing that mattered was that we were here together.

# 19

## DARCY

When I lean in for a goodbye kiss, Anya puts up a hand.

"Hold on," she says. "I need to tell you something about to-morrow's dinner. I've been avoiding it all night, and I can't let you show up without knowing. I already know you'll say you don't believe me, but I promise you, it's true."

"What is it? You're not . . ." I try on a laugh that doesn't fit, falling off me like oversized clothing, pooling at my feet, and leaving me exposed in my confusion. "You're not a . . . *witch.*"

It comes out like a curse word. A sin. It's not any of those things. Because it's not real.

Except for the fact that she fixed Maddie's wings.

And she fixed my gnome.

And she dresses like . . .

Well, she dresses like a witch.

Sitting in her aunt's car in the dim of the alley, just a sin-gle streetlamp illuminating us both, Anya searches my face for a reaction.

"You're an *actual* witch?" This time it's a question. My last chance at understanding the world as it's been.

Anya reaches up to grab one of the dried flowers her aunt keeps inside her car. She picks a rose that's dark red and so dehydrated that it looks ready to crumble to pieces at her touch. The gesture seems out of place. Is she about to hand it to me as some sort of strange joke?

Instead she does something even stranger. She releases the stem of the flower and holds just the petals. When she closes her eyes, she *really* closes them, like she's gone into a deep sleep.

Her breaths get so drawn out that I start to count them—six seconds in and six seconds out. I'm so transfixed by her face, calm and serene, that I almost miss what's happening in her hands.

The rose has begun to bloom again. What was once dull and crinkled is now teeming with life as something like dust whirls around the air. Anya remains still, like she's cast in amber.

My brain struggles to make sense of it all, thinking of the parlor tricks I've learned through my years at Pam's Paints. Perhaps in the time I was looking at her face, she was able to swap out the flower? Maybe the rose is made that way, and there's a button she's pressed where she's transformed it?

Or . . .

Maybe, just maybe . . .

"You're an actual witch," I say.

This time I believe myself.

This time it's real.

Anya opens her eyes. She moves her hands down to hold the stem again, displaying the rose. It looks new as ever—a rich, deep red that I can tell even from here would feel like velvet on my skin.

Anya tucks it back into its place along the seam of the sunroof. "This is from my parents' wedding. Aunt Cal thinks it's good luck to have it, because my mom grew it. Mom has a gift for gardening, so it's way more resilient than your usual rose. I have a bouquet of them in my room too. They've always been my practice flower. They've died and been revived more times than I can count. Because I'm a mender. I can bring things back to life."

"Your mom is a witch too?" I ask.

Anya looks at me expectantly, waiting for me to keep unraveling this.

"Aunt Cal," I whisper. Of course Aunt Cal is also a witch. There's never been a woman more like a witch in all of Fableview. But up until now I didn't believe that witches had actual, tangible powers.

"Everyone on my maternal side has the gift," Anya tells me. "I don't have my dad's last name. My dad doesn't even have my dad's last name anymore, actually. I was born to be a member of the Doyle coven. I'm sorry I lied the last time you asked me."

"To be fair, you told me the truth a few times before that," I say. "Would be kind of hard for me to be upset about it. I just . . . I can't believe it's real."

The joy that's started to flood my system reminds me of what I used to feel late at night on Christmas Eve, looking out my bedroom window, trying to catch Santa on my balcony.

*Fableview's magic is real.*

I can't help the tear that falls down my cheek.

"Oh no. I didn't mean to upset you," Anya says.

"You haven't," I tell her, smiling through my crying. "I promise. I just have seventeen years' worth of Fableview stories to work through now."

Anya kisses my cheek. "Take your time with it. If we have to cancel the dinner, I understand."

"We're definitely not canceling," I say. "I'm not passing up my chance to eat with a family of witches."

*Witches.*

Real, actual witches.

By the time I make it back to my room, I still have that same warm sensation. I used to get it on Halloween too, I realize. Before it became too much of my responsibility. This pure contentment and wonder has finally come home to me.

Grace picks up on the second ring. "What's wrong?"

"Nothing's wrong," I tell her, hearing the smile in my voice.

"*Stop,*" she whispers. She knows, because of course she knows. We could have this entire conversation without me even telling her what happened. And as much as I love that about us, I have so much I want to say. Explain. Understand. And Grace is the only one in the world I trust with it.

"So . . . yeah. Anya and me," I start as confirmation.

"I'm *dying,*" Grace replies.

It's been so long since we've called each other with the kind of news we need to whisper about. It makes me nostalgic for our middle school days, when we'd gossip about who looked at us a certain way, obsessing over a lingering stare, a brush of a hand. So much of the last year has been about my future.

Part of me has liked that change in status. It's all been so adult, so focused on who I will become, that it hasn't given me much room to just *be*. For this I'm right here—just a seventeen-year-old girl on the phone with her best friend, half tucked under her covers after having snuck out of the house to meet her crush.

"I could tell something happened after she won her semi-final," Grace says. "She was so determined for the finals. Like she'd been reborn."

"We kissed," I confirm.

"*I knew it*," she says, full of satisfaction. "Oh, this is so good."

"It isn't . . . random of me? Or unexpected?"

Grace quiets, all her frenetic enthusiasm distilled into one slow breath. "Why would I ever care?" she asks, genuinely. "You already know that I'll date anyone. I would never think it's weird that you're with a girl."

I *do* know this. It's never been an actual worry of mine. But we've never discussed it before either. There's something comforting about getting her confirmation anyway. What I really needed to know is that some changes don't require any pushback. Some growth is good exactly as it is.

"I sort of didn't, like, fully realize before her," I say. "That I could like girls. I've always thought they were cute. But I've never had any girl who actually lived in Fableview who I wanted to do anything with."

"Of course not," Grace replies with her pitch-perfect understanding. "We've been stuck with the same dating pool our entire lives. No one's gotten surprisingly hot around here since Parker Holt."

Everything always comes back to Parker Holt for Grace. It's kind of beautiful, the way she can always find a way to connect anything in her life to them. It's something I haven't fully understood before now. Because I've never seen a reason to connect things to Kyle Holtzenberg, other than my wish to leave this town altogether.

Now I get it. I understand how Grace can filter everyone else's experiences through her connection to Parker. Even here on the phone, I keep running my hand over my leg, remembering the stars Anya traced there. I feel so full of all this newness, desperate to dissect it.

Grace lets me. With excitement I replay everything for her, all the way back to that first exchange outside the art shop when Anya crashed our paint night. We pick apart these memories, climb inside them like they're cocoons, living in the past until it butterflies us to the present, to the bright and vivid now of an hour ago, me and Anya atop her aunt's Volkswagen.

"Do you think you'll go to the Fall Ball together?" Grace asks.

It's the first real question about the future instead of the past, and it startles me. "I hadn't even thought of that."

"Please," Grace says in a get-real way.

"Okay, obviously I've thought about the Fall Ball, but I haven't thought about going with Anya," I say. "That would be . . ."

I imagine it, the same way I once saw my future with Kyle Holtzenberg when he lifted me up last year. I try to see Anya and me together under the purple lights. Would she want to dance with me? Would she like it? The fact that I can't quite picture it is exciting. It's a future I don't know, another unknown I might want to chase.

"Maybe I'll ask her," I say, feeling the fizzy thrill of possibility take root. "I'm going to a dinner with her family tomorrow."

"Good. You can find out if they're actually witches," Grace says. "It would explain Maddie's wings. And the ceramics."

In all my shock at Anya's reveal, I forgot to ask if I could tell Grace the truth too. Until then, I'll play my usual part.

"I'll definitely find out if they're witches for you," I say. "Once we finish dessert, I'll grab a broomstick and ask if they have any interest in joining me on the roof."

"Perfect," Grace says. "Then you guys can fly to the Trinity knot in the woods and sprinkle another year of good fortune over Fableview a little earlier than usual. We're close enough to Halloween that I'm sure it'll still be effective."

"Won't we need our basset hound to guide us to the correct spot?" I ask.

"The basset hound will be there spiritually," Grace says. "Because the basset hound may or may not be going on a date with Parker Holt tomorrow . . ."

We're off to the races again, Grace explaining to me how Parker apologized to her at the apple orchard. How they're really different this time. She's giddy, excited.

For the first time, I don't feel like talking Grace out of it, warning her of the future hurts. The inevitable pain. It's nice to live in the right now.

We talk until our voices are hoarse. And then we keep talking, long pauses for each of us when we accidentally fall asleep. Finally, at some ungodly hour, Grace is openly snoring, and I end the call.

I look at the picture of Anya and me atop her aunt's Volkswagen. *Who can we become to each other?* I wonder, zooming in on different parts of the image as if it might have the answer. But it doesn't. It just is, perfect and fleeting and totally foreign.

*Finally*, I think with a little smile. *I can paint her. My witch.*

# 10 Days Until Halloween

# 20

## ANYA

The Keller family arrives at 6:23 p.m., knocking three times on the front door. "Hello! We're here!" Mr. Keller calls out.

My parents are upstairs, still getting ready. Aunt Cal looks at the clock on the wall, studying the time as if it might move faster with her attention on it. "We set a time because we meant it," she says.

"They're only seven minutes early," I say.

"And seven minutes can be a very long time, depending on the circumstances."

"We brought cupcakes!" Mrs. Keller announces.

Aunt Cal lets out a long, theatrical grunt.

When she doesn't move, I stand up. My whole face burns, nerves and embarrassment fighting a winless war inside me as I make the long processional to the front door.

There are animal bones atop Aunt Cal's mantel, long-dead pets of hers that she took to a taxidermist to be cleaned by dermestid beetles, now forever immortalized in various strange, skeletal positions. She has a cat standing on its hind legs, batting at an imaginary fly. A snake positioned as if ready to bite. A ferret mid-growl. The entryway wall is covered with moths pinned by their wings, captured inside shadow boxes, mixed in with portraits of our dead relatives and moody renderings of the Cailleach, an old crone known in Irish mythology to rule over the winter months.

The Kellers love Halloween in the *candy corn hat and fake spiderweb draped across a bush* kind of way. It's never creepy in their version of Fableview. Aunt Cal's house feels like a mausoleum, in contrast. A tribute to the dead, or "life after life," as she likes to say.

Never has the contrast been clearer than when the Kellers file inside one by one. Mr. Keller has opted to wear a pumpkin tie atop a bright orange button-down, carrying cupcakes frosted in the same shade. Mrs. Keller is wearing a white turtleneck with a purple sleeveless vest over it, tiny bedsheet ghosts sewn on to match her ghost earrings. They look like comic book characters trapped inside the wrong story, wandering a haunted house when they're meant to be tossing out lollipops from a parade float.

Darcy comes in last, holding a jug of apple cider and wearing an apologetic grin. She has on a short, flowy dress in a lovely shade of lilac, with a V-cut neckline that emphasizes her double-chain gold necklace. It's a crescent moon and a star, one layer resting near the hollow of her throat and the other hovering above the top seam of the dress, daring my eyes to look lower.

"Sorry we're early." She's close enough that I can smell her lotion, buttery sweet and irresistible. "I tried to get them to wait in the car."

"I'm not personally offended, but I can't speak for my aunt," I say back.

Darcy gives my hand one quick squeeze. My face betrays my cool, showing all my breathless excitement. "It's okay. You can smile."

My cheeks pull back on her command. "So long as you don't tell anyone at school I'm capable of it."

"I'd never." She leans in close. "But can I tell them you're a witch? I forgot to ask that last night. Grace already thinks you are."

"Of course she does," I say. "For now, though, let's keep it between you and me."

*Because I won't be a witch much longer.* I push the thought away.

Aunt Cal swoops into the front room, where we've gathered. Her patchwork jacket trails behind her. Instead of delivering her own greeting, she waits for the Kellers to announce themselves, not responding until Darcy apologizes for their early arrival.

"We're so sorry we're early," she says.

Aunt Cal gives her a curt nod. Then she turns around, heading toward the dining room, the long, dramatic swoop of her jacket seeming to say, *Follow if you must.*

My parents come down the stairs and exchange hellos with the Kellers, giving hugs and talking about general Fableview chatter. Darcy and I immediately sequester ourselves, sitting down side by side at the long dining table.

Darcy places her hand atop my leg under the table. I lean in to her. Another game for us to play. How many ways can we touch each other without anyone noticing?

"This place is cool," she says.

There are stacks of books on witchcraft, family tomes and regular fare, everywhere the eye can see. Crystals and melted candles cover every surface that isn't adorned with relics and offerings. "It's very Cal," I say, hoping that somehow explains it all.

"Reminds me of you too," she replies. "Witchy."

My heart leaps at the comment. "I can't believe I'm the one who's made a believer out of Darcy Keller."

"A powerful witch indeed," she teases, stroking her thumb along the top of my thigh.

My mom excuses herself to bring out the plates of food, ending our ability to keep ourselves together. The adults choose their spots along the table, and the dinner begins in earnest.

"It's good to see you, Cal," Mrs. Keller starts, even though she's already said a form of this without me and Darcy involved. "And, Rhonda. It's been years."

They know each other, which makes sense, because Cal's lived here a very long time, and the Kellers have too. It's still strange to witness this connection, like it's incorrect somehow that these two worlds intermingled long before my inclusion.

I wonder again about Piper Blake's dad. If Darcy's parents know about Cal's breakup with him. There must be stories between all of them. Lore that could take up hours of this meal. That's how this town operates.

"We'd love to see you at the shop more," Mrs. Keller says, and Cal actually looks down at her hands, bashful. It's so rare to see—Cal uncomfortable in a way she can't hide behind her stony glances.

I hate that I recognize myself in it. All those times I thought I was hiding away were exactly when I was the most exposed. It's braver to own the discomfort than it is to act like it doesn't exist.

"I stopped in recently," Cal says. "Looks very nice in there."

"You did? I wish I knew! We'd have loved to catch up."

"Yeah, she was there at the costume parade," Darcy tells her parents.

"We're old friends," Mr. Keller says.

A tense moment passes, something decided among the adults that isn't for us to discuss here. It must be about Piper Blake's dad and Cal. Since Darcy and Piper are friends, the Kellers are probably good friends with the infamous Mark Blake too.

"So!" Mr. Keller says good-naturedly, looking down the table at me. "What's next for you, Anya? Any plans for after high school?"

I shift in my seat, acutely aware of the fabric of my shirt, the sweat that's pooling underneath my armpits, seeping through the black.

"Tough to say," I tell him, meaning it.

My mom laughs, taking the opportunity to pat my head. "Anya has a home with any of us in the family, but I know she's been loving it here in Fableview. She'd probably be thrilled to stick around."

Sweat.

Dripping.

"Music to our ears!" Mr. Keller says back. "That's exactly what our Darcy's planning to do too. She's taking over our art shop for us when we retire. Hopefully next year, if all goes well, but certainly in the next two!"

"How about that?" my mom says in amazement. She gazes

across me to look at Darcy, offering her a genuine smile of excitement. "You must be thrilled."

"We're ecstatic," her dad says. "I'm sure you know how badly the Holtzenbergs want control of the Halloween festivities. We're happy to be able to keep it in the family."

"The Holtzenbergs still want in on that?" Mom asks. "Goodness, the people around here really don't change, do they?"

This makes Darcy laugh. It's a bitter, uncomfortable sound, drawing all the attention to her. "Actually," she says, "I might go to college out of state." She takes a huge bite of her ravioli.

The ripple of shock moves in slow-motion, bouncing off me and sailing down the table until it reaches her parents. Her dad cocks his head to the side, almost like he's shaking water out of his ear, confident he hasn't heard her right. Her mom leans forward, elbows on the table. Darcy holds herself up straight, continuing to look my mom in the eye as she chews.

"That's probably for the best," Aunt Cal says, pulling the focus off Darcy for her first offering of the meal. She sits at the head of the table, looking straight forward.

If anyone other than me had a sense of what was going on, it's lost now. Only I understand the message Cal is sending, and all I can do is hope she doesn't feel the need to share that message aloud.

Darcy, still embracing her bold rebellion, says, "Why's that?"

"Because there's no way you can be Anya's protector now that you're her romantic interest."

There it is. Out in the open.

If Darcy's statement about college tilted us sideways, this flips us upside down completely.

"Protector?" Darcy asks.

"Romantic interest?" says my mom.

"College?" Darcy's parents ask in unison.

Darcy and I exchange a look, trying to see in each other's face what we think is going on. There are a dozen Ping-Pong balls bouncing around us, at us, through us, and the easiest way to solve this is to catch and handle just one.

Just us.

"Can we be excused?" I direct this question to my dad, because he hasn't contributed to the conversation so far, and he's most likely to let me escape the pressure of this situation.

He gives me a solemn nod, and I take Darcy's hand.

# 21

# DARCY

The spiral staircase creaks with every step, groaning under the frantic pace we've adopted. In the attic, the walls lean in until they reach a point, covering us in a triangle of wooden slats. There is only a bed, a clothes rack, and a mirrored dresser up here. A single black sheet doubles as a curtain covering the sole window. The clothes rack shows Anya's limited collection of black apparel, with a small chest beside it that must contain her underwear. I don't know why my mind goes there, to wondering what she wears beneath her clothes. It must be my burning desire to get further under her skin. To keep peeling back the layers of her and know more, more, more.

Up here, alone with her, I can't help but remember what it felt like to lie on top of her. How she was so warm, comfortable but unfamiliar. It's all I have to hold me in place as I make sense of the last few minutes—telling my parents about college, then Anya's aunt mentioning something about me being a protector. And a romantic interest.

"Every coven is different," Anya starts. There's a pronounced waver in her voice. "In our family, the initiation happens on your eighteenth birthday. In order to join officially, you need to name a mortal protector who promises to look after you. My family thinks that will be you, because I told them it would."

She must see the way this startles me, how my face can't help but contort into something frustrated, put off.

"I had to say *something*," she continues. "They knew I didn't have friends anywhere I'd lived, and the clock was ticking on my choice. So I said you, because you were the first person I thought of. I'm always thinking of you, in some way or another."

I want to be charmed, but my confusion's winning out.

"My parents immediately wanted to meet you," she says. "So I just kept getting further and further into the lie. But Aunt Cal has a rule against romantic interests being named as protectors, and somehow, she knows about us. I think she had a vision about it."

"When were you going to tell me I was your protector?" I ask. It comes out like an accusation.

Maybe it is. There's a part of me that's hurt. Deeply. Not by her being a witch. But by the plan she's made for me—a plan in which I've had no say. A plan that would keep me here in Fableview, when she knows that's the last thing I really want.

"You've had all this time to talk about it with me. If you were worried about someone else overhearing, we couldn't have been more alone out by the creek."

The memory burns now, fire licking the edges of what was once so perfect. The truth has changed every interaction, darkened all the sweetness.

Anya's stoic. It's a stark contrast to the tears streaking down my face, fast and hot, and my hands, which move along with my every word. I need to keep myself in motion, because to stop is to fall apart, and I'm not ready for that. "All this time, you've been making up my future without my input. You of all people should know why that would hurt."

"I do," she says, still unmoving. "I wish I had a better reason. I never thought you'd actually do it. I just had to give them an answer. I was scared."

"I'm also scared!" I argue, my voice rising against my will. "All of this is new to me too. Just because I dated Kyle Holtzenberg doesn't mean I understand how to do this with you any more than you know how to do it with me. But I was the one who assumed you'd know me enough to know I'd want to be included in any plans you were making, even if you didn't expect those plans to come true. It turns out I was completely wrong."

Her face falls. I wish it didn't give me any satisfaction, but the wounded animal inside my heart appreciates that she's got her own wounds to lick.

"I'm so sorry," she says.

"I know you are," I say back. "But it doesn't change that it happened. It doesn't undo it."

My dad appears in Anya's room, the concern on his face a strange contrast to his silly pumpkin tie. "We have to go," he says to Anya. "Thank you for having us."

I make a move to protest. There is still so much we need to sort out. We can't leave it *here*.

But my dad says three words he's never spoken to me before, and they're so foreign, so strange, I have to ask him to repeat himself, just to make sure I've understood him right.

"Darcy, you're grounded."

## 22

# ANYA

Mom leans her head against the doorway in her sad-puppy way. "Honey, are you sure you don't want to come downstairs with us? We'd love to spend some time with you."

"I don't feel well," I tell her, which is true, but it's more of an existential ache than it is a real one.

She comes to my bed and puts her hand on my forehead.

Sometimes I forget my mom is my mom. All this time away from her, living with different relatives, I've spent it existing to be trained, soaking up knowledge and taking in the culture of all these safe-haven towns, looking for what will one day be my home. I've lost the sense that someone should care for me. That I don't have to do anything to earn this attention. Show off my best tricks to make sure she knows I'm worth her time.

"You *do* feel warm," Mom says.

Now I don't know who is lying to who. Except maybe I am sick. Lovesick, I guess.

She sits herself on the edge of my bed. "Would you like to talk about it?"

What a question. Kryptonite really. I expect to conjure up my most disapproving face—channeling the proud legacy of every sullen Doyle witch who has come before me. I find myself leaning into Mom instead. Placing my head on her shoulder.

"It's okay, sweetie," Mom says, rubbing my shoulders. "I'm here."

I start to cry. It's a fountain, long suppressed, now overflowing. Or water breaking through a dam. Poetry has never been my strength. If it was, these are the kinds of feelings I would write about.

"I can't join our coven," I say through heaving sniffles. "I don't have anyone to be my protector. I have no friends. Darcy was never my friend in the first place. And Aunt Cal is right. Even if she wanted to be my protector, I wouldn't want her to be. It's not what we are to each other. But without her, I have no one."

"Honey, I know," Mom says.

"What?" I ask, wiping my face.

"Your father and I came out here a little early in the hopes of figuring something out for you." Through my confusion, my mom keeps talking, cupping her hand under my chin. "I've known all along, dear. You may be secretive, but that doesn't mean you're good at lying."

I'm so used to going unnoticed. *Feeling* unnoticed. I think again of Cal at dinner. How I'd caught her trying to hide but found myself capable of knowing exactly what it was she hid from. Still, it didn't occur to me that my mom could see through it all too. That she could see *me*.

"As you can tell, we know a good amount of people in town from seeing Cal over the years and my time spent here with your grandma when she'd come to visit," Mom says. "We thought maybe we could come out and find someone for you. Make a few calls. I'm sure the Holtzenbergs would be interested."

This is enough to get my tears to stop.

"*Kyle Holtzenberg*," I say, like my mom will know how ridiculous this suggestion is just by the sound of his name.

Judging by the look she gives me, she seems to know. Still, gently, she says, "We have to come up with someone, honey. And if he's willing, we're not in the position to turn him down, are we? And at least he's not someone you're romantically involved with, right?"

"*Mom,*" I say, horrified.

On my dresser, tucked into the corner of my mirror, is the calendar of events Darcy gave me. Mom gets up to grab it, looking at the check marks I've placed next to everything I've gone to. "You went to all of these?"

"Yeah," I say, my sadness reignited at the sight of it. "I've been to all that stuff, and I *still* don't have a friend."

She probably means to use this as proof of my life, to remind me how I've been putting myself out there and trying, but it's just another reminder of my failure.

I haven't made a friend. Haven't made a plan for a life outside of being a witch. The thought of her calling in a favor to someone in town is so embarrassing to me, I want my tears to make an ocean where I can live in a boat of my own despair. Kyle Holtzenberg getting dragged to my coven initiation to pledge his lifelong allegiance to me.

Please.

"I don't want you to fix it for me," I tell my mom. "I want to have figured it out on my own. And I hate that I haven't. I want to change, and I just can't. I'm not ready."

My mom, usually one for words, knows there is nothing more to say. This is a fight I've won. And maybe with time I will eventually surrender to the devastating pits of embarrassment that will come from having someone like Kyle Holtzenberg at my initiation because my family paid him off. The first person in our coven to have an arranged friendship.

For now, my mom comes back to hold me as I cry.

"I didn't mean to hurt her," I say.

"I know you didn't, sweetie," Mom replies. She thinks I mean Darcy, and part of me does. But there's another part of me that's thinking about Julia, all those years ago. How even though she was awful and she manipulated me, I still let her down.

At first I think Mom is holding me so tight that she's surrounding me on all sides. But then I hear another voice, a little sharper.

"Heartbreak hurts."

It's Aunt Cal. She's crawled up onto the other side of my bed to hold me too.

"There's no way out but through," she says.

"Is this what you saw in your vision?" I ask her.

"It doesn't matter what I saw," she tells me. I've never heard her voice this soothing. "What matters is that you know we're here. You won't go through this alone."

And that's how we stay for the rest of the night.

# 23

## DARCY

My parents have been disappointed in me, and they've been frustrated with me, but for the first time in my life, they are truly *mad* at me.

"We're holding an emergency family meeting," Mom says, gesturing for me to take a seat on our couch.

It would be easy to slump down and listen. In all my other, less serious offenses—which have been few and far between—that's what I'd do. But this is different. This I haven't earned at all.

"I want to say something first." I hold my spot in the space between the living room and the hallway. "I think I have a right to want something outside of Fableview. I love it here. Really. You guys are great parents. And I have great friends. It's a great town. But everything I do is for *you*. I work at *your* business. I sign up for *your* activities. None of it feels like it's truly *mine*."

They look at me with that same startled expression I've been seeing all month, like their beloved daughter has been swapped with a changeling.

"We hoped meeting Anya would help us understand all this," Mom tells me. "But now we know her family wants to rope you into her magic. And it's time for us to take more serious measures to intervene."

"Why are you talking about her like she's dangerous? She told me my grandma was best friends with her grandma."

"She was," my dad tells me. "My mother was best friends with Agnes Doyle. They were inseparable right up until Grandma died. Called each other on the phone almost every night. I never understood why Agnes didn't move here, but that didn't seem to stop the two of them from staying close."

"So you guys knew Anya was a witch?" I ask.

"We live in *Fableview*," Mom says. "A lot of people here are witches."

"Why didn't you ever tell me that they were *real*?" I ask. "I thought they were like Santa Claus. And you guys have always treated the magic of Fableview like a business decision, not a reality."

"It's a complicated subject," Dad says. "We knew from your grandma that the Doyle coven prefers to operate under the radar. The whole reason they have protectors is to help keep them safe."

"Safe from what? Our town is obsessed with magic! Everyone would be thrilled to have them practicing out in the open. I've seen what Anya can do. It would amaze people."

"Magic is something all regular people want to believe in," Dad says. "They want to think they could be witches too. That's what we sell them on, that hope. If they learn that some people have actual, genuine powers, they stop hoping that they might have them too. Like your mother said, Cal and Anya aren't the only witches in town. The Blakes have powers too."

"*Piper?*" I shake my head. They're sidetracking me, like they're so good at doing. "So what's the problem with Anya, then? Why couldn't I be her protector if I wanted to?" Who knows why I'm asking this? I don't want the job. But this whole situation is ridiculous. "Is it that she and I are . . . that we kissed?"

"No!" Mom hurries out.

"Absolutely not!" Dad practically falls forward with this assurance. "We are so happy to see you living as your true self. We don't care about gender. We just care about *you*. But you're telling us that you want to be her protector at the same time that you're saying that you want to go to college out of state. How can both of those things be true?"

He's got me there. "That's what makes all this so confusing," I say, close to tears already. "It's just that everyone wants to decide what I get to do with my life," I continue. "All I've ever wanted to do is make you guys proud, but I also want a chance to at least learn what my life could be like if I didn't live here. And maybe I'd hate it. Maybe I'd want to come back after a week. But I want to at least *try*. Anya was the first person to ever make me think I could. And then it turned out that she wanted something from me too."

My parents' hurt is evident, and it only hurts *me* worse to see it.

"C'mon. You've written out my whole life plan without consulting me," I say. It feels good to empty this out. For once to say this as it is and not pretend I mean something other than what I say. "I can't believe that Anya did it to me too, telling her family I planned to be her protector here in Fableview. Even if she didn't actually mean it, it still hurts. Everyone wants to give me responsibilities, knowing I can take anything on, but no one ever includes me in the conversation about what that responsibility will be."

"You're still grounded," Dad tells me.

This takes both Mom and me by surprise. He's always been the more amenable one in my eyes, the one more likely to see things my way. Whenever I have a request for a later curfew or a need for a new phone, he's the one I ask. But he's harsh now, unflinching in the face of my raw, wounded truth.

"You didn't give us a say in your plan either," he continues. "You've had plenty of time to discuss college with us, and instead of doing that, you sprang it on us with no notice. We were at a friendly meal with a group of people we barely know. No matter how you were feeling inside, that wasn't an appropriate setting. We are your parents. We love you. We want the best for you. But we want to be a part of the conversation too."

"That's exactly what you did to me with the shop!" I argue back, my hysteria rising. It all feels so deeply unfair.

"You're right," Mom says, placing a gentle hand on Dad's arm.

"Him or me?" I ask.

"Both of you. We're all stressed. We've taken on too much, and we're not spending enough time on what matters. That's what my mom used to tell me. Don't forget the people who matter. And we've been forgetting each other."

"You're the ones who made us this busy," I can't help but say.

"I know. But we can't ever be too busy for our own family." She looks to Dad, waiting for him to get on board.

They have a stony exchange with only their eyes, doing their silent parental thing until Dad loosens his tie and says, "We'll ground ourselves too."

"You'll . . . what?"

"We'll stay home with you," he explains. "As of right now, the entire Keller family is under house arrest."

This is supposed to be some kind of compromise that makes it better. That's what they seem to think, giving each other proud-parent looks, like they've really handled this well. But they haven't handled anything. They haven't really heard me.

"It doesn't matter what we do," I tell them, storming toward my bedroom. "Because I already applied to a college out of state. And if I get in, I'm definitely going there."

With that, I slam my door shut, closing them out of this discussion for the rest of the night.

# 9 Days Until Halloween

# 24

## ANYA

Right as my mind is about to drift off, finally surrendering me to the sweet mercy of sleep after the previous night's terrible, restless thrashing—me unable to stop replaying the horrible conversation with Darcy—there are two loud thuds and one distinct cry of frustration.

*"Shit!"*

I startle out of bed. There's an intruder in my room. I need to learn martial arts or something. Glares won't cut it in hand-to-hand combat.

But a fight won't be necessary. At least I hope not.

Grace Manalo is currently splayed across my floor. She's wearing all black, down to two smudges underneath each eye, with a bandana tied around her forehead, holding back her braids.

"Did you just break in through my window?" I ask her.

She blows an exasperated puff of air toward her face, moving a stray wisp of hair out of her eyes. "I don't know your number, and you have your DMs turned off on everything. How else do you expect people to get in contact with you?"

"Knocking on the front door would've done it."

"I tried that. Your aunt told me you were in mourning and not to disturb you. Which I would've taken as a no, except I met your mom, who told me you'd actually love some company. Neither of them could decide who was more right, so I was stuck there for a while."

"But you're dressed like a burglar. Or a linebacker."

"Haven't you learned the value of a costume in this town?" she asks. "I'm cultivating a sense of intentional whimsy, Doyle. Life's a performance. It's time you start tap-dancing on the stage a little bit."

"Is breaking into my house a performance or an actual crime?"

"I'm not loving your tone," Grace warns. "Besides, your mom gave me a ladder. She told me you always leave this window open and that it's just big enough for me to fit through. Which reminds me!" Grace walks back to the window, sticking her head out. "Thanks, Rhonda! I got in just as easily as you said I would! Appreciate you!" She blows my mom a kiss.

This whole thing is absurd. But it's also oddly moving. "No one has ever climbed a ladder to reach me," I say.

"Yeah, well, I'm an exceptional person," Grace responds. "It's not really news if you've been paying attention."

And she's right. It isn't news. I can imagine a hundred scenarios where Grace would climb a ladder for Darcy, or probably even for the famous Parker Holt. I just never would have imagined a scenario where she'd do it for me.

"Enough about my fantastic qualities," Grace says. "We need to talk about how you're a witch."

She gives me that same look I've seen so many times before, like she's always known this. And it seems as though she has. Like how Cal isn't hiding whenever she tries to be silent and removed. But all these years of trying to hide has made me rusty at accepting this truth as something capable of being shared.

Grace runs her finger across my clothes rack. "The all-black thing is kind of obvious, isn't it? I guess I can appreciate commitment to a theme, though."

"Maybe I'm cultivating a sense of intentional whimsy," I say.

She moves to my dresser, smirking as she examines my crystals and knickknacks, tokens I've collected from my years spread out across different towns and different members of my family.

"I've known all along," she says.

Those words thrust me back through time, an echo of my past that I've never been able to escape. At once, I'm not seventeen. I'm twelve, living with my Uncle Edward and Aunt Paula. Grace isn't Grace. She's Julia Daniels. The girl I thought would be my protector.

"I know you're a witch," Julia had told me. *"I've known all along."*

The memory has real determination. In all my years of attempting to dismiss it, it's only ever gotten stronger. And now here is Grace, echoing Julia's words, and I have to fight the urge to plug my ears and curl up into a ball, knowing Julia herself is poking around somewhere, still believing her own version of events.

"You can save my grandpa," Julia had said. Her eyes went hard as she clenched her jaw, folding her arms across her chest.

"I really don't know how," I said. I was desperate for her to believe me. To make her understand. And even if I did, all I'd ever heard from my mentors was that Doyle witches don't mess with the natural order of human life.

"Of course you do," she pressed. "You're a *mender*. I already know. I heard you talking about it. So do something."

She said "mender" like an insult. Like a curse.

"I can close a paper cut sometimes, but I'm not even very good at it. I can't cure your grandpa's cancer," I told her.

"You really are a witch," she said then, her angry determination softening for a single moment. She'd told me she already knew. She'd lied, and I'd walked into her trap of confirmation by accident. "You're not even gonna do the right thing? You're not gonna help the one person who's bothered to put up with you here?"

"I'm really sorry," I said, tears brimming against my will. "I wish I could. But I don't even think it's allowed. No. I'm sure it isn't. My mom already told me that. I can't mess with fate like that."

"Whatever." Julia stomped across the room to pick up her coat. "If you can't do that for me, I don't even know why we're friends."

Her grandpa died a few weeks later. I tried to be the bigger person and express my condolences. And she blamed me. Told me that if I'd just been a good person, I could have helped her. But I was selfish. I didn't think about other people at all. Only about myself. I lied about my powers. About what I could do. I used her.

Those were the last words she'd willingly said to my face. The rest of my time there was filled with insults muttered under her breath as I walked past her and judgmental laughs from everyone in my grade whenever the teachers made me speak in public. Until I couldn't take it anymore and called my mom, begging her to let me leave.

"Darcy already knows," I say now to Grace, squeezing my eyes shut to stop myself from having to see this again. To live this kind of moment twice. "But I messed everything up anyway. So don't worry, you don't have to embarrass me any more than I already have been."

My own breathing, rapid and tight, is the only audible thing in the room. Grace is waiting, forcing me to open my eyes, to look at her and take this on the chin.

When I do, she flops onto the edge of my bed. "I really had you wrong. Like, I already knew that, but now I get it. You're not brooding in a boring, obvious way. You're, like, really wounded."

I shrug.

"I relate," she continues. "People don't see me as wounded either. But I'm actually really sensitive. I'm just good at doing it with a smile, you know?"

It's not unusual to find myself wordless. It's most of my life. What's stranger is my need to say something. To want to talk to Grace.

"You've never struck me as someone who doesn't have feelings," I tell her.

"Of course not. Everyone just sees me as dramatic, though. Like my emotions are oversized for the sake of spectacle. My soul is actually a lot more like your gothic, cobwebbed aesthetic than anyone would ever expect."

I bet another person would laugh at this. Grace's delivery is so big, so *dramatic*, as she would say, that it's easy to see her as unserious. But her whole life is an exercise in taking things more seriously than anyone else ever has. She's shown up to my house dressed as a burglar without a hint of irony. And her thing with reptiles. She regularly wears clothing covered in images of snakes or lizards or crocodiles.

"Even though my own heart has been unjustly stomped on more than once, I'm a romantic," she tells me. "Which is why, when they gave me one good apology speech, I took them back."

"Parker Holt," I say, the only thing I know for sure in this whole mess.

"The one and only. Anyway, Parker and me is not what matters right now. Although it *is* very interesting. It's for another time. I know about what happened with you and Darcy, obviously."

It *is* obvious, I guess, that Darcy would tell her best friend. If I had a friend to tell, I'd have done the same thing. And honestly, I can't imagine a better audience than Grace.

"Normally I'd just coach her through the breakup, because it does build character," Grace continues. "Even her little stint with Kyle Holtzenberg gave her some necessary shading. But I want to help you."

"You're here to help . . . *me*?"

She makes a waving gesture. "Have I not made that clear? I misjudged you, and I'm owning that. You're a good person, and you're good for Darcy. So I want to help you win her back."

I want to argue that I haven't *lost* Darcy. But I know I have. I've blown up her life like a dynamite stick, and she hasn't texted me back since the dinner. She didn't look at me today in school either, and not in our usual *we don't know really each other* way.

She *avoided* me.

"She's pretty mad at you," Grace goes on, confirming what I've already felt. "You really should've told her about the whole protector thing."

"I wanted to. It just took so long to get her to believe I am an actual witch that I forgot all about the protector thing."

"I know. I tried to tell her you were a witch too," she says. "Before you came along, she never really embraced magic as reality. That's something you can't exactly convince someone of unless you can do it yourself, and unfortunately, I don't have powers like you do. But things just go over Darcy's head sometimes anyway. She didn't realize how long she'd liked you either."

My cheeks burn. This is precious information, rarefied intel, and I know it. I feel like I'm not supposed to want to hear more, but I can't help myself. "How long has she liked me, exactly?"

"You made a wrong move," Grace says, ever the diplomatic best friend. "But we can definitely fix it."

"How?"

"The haunted carnival." She plucks the schedule from my mirror, inspecting it. "I see here you already know about it. I'd tell you it's a big deal, but everything is a big deal this month. So it's just *another* big deal."

"I'm beginning to learn that," I tell her.

"I've been opposed to this whole change-the-town campaign. Recent circumstances have swayed me." She plops down on my bed again. "Darcy's always wanted to make the carnival spookier. Everything we do in Fableview is so tame, and every time we go to the carnival, she says there should be at least one place where it gets scary. I know my little sister Maddie would love that too. She's desperate for some real horror in this town. Who better to create some scares than a real-life witch, right?

And if that makes a certain reformed skeptic swoon, well . . . isn't that what us hard-hearted romantics do?"

"I mostly, um . . . fix broken things," I tell her, feeling unworthy of this speech, and this situation, and even the title of a romantic.

"Then let's fix your broken heart, girl. C'mon. You can't wallow any more than you already have. Please. It's not a good look." She makes her way to the window again. "Are you in or not?"

"You haven't said what we're going to do."

She smiles. Sly. Knowing. "Don't worry about that part. I've already got our costumes picked out. All I need is confirmation that you'll participate."

"I'm in," I say with a shaky breath.

"Right answer."

She leaves my room the same way she came in, through the ladder at my window, with my mom holding it steady for her so she can get safely to the ground.

# 7 Days Until Halloween

# 25

# DARCY

Going to the haunted carnival on Friday night has always been my and Grace's personal tradition. Something about sitting through school during the day—giddy, restless—then spending hours getting ready afterward, putting on our best makeup and our cutest nonthemed clothes, is the height of sophistication to us. The contrast is the point. A regular, boring day of school into a long, eventful night in the middle of a cornfield.

The carnival runs later than any other event on the Halloween schedule, open until midnight for the entire weekend. Staying out that late in public, with permission from everyone in the town, adds to the sophistication. Anything can happen at the haunted carnival.

That fateful year that Kyle Holtzenberg and I first got together, we held hands on the carnival's Ferris wheel. It was the most illicit, overwhelming thrill of my sixth-grade life. The action of it—linking hands with someone else, declaring our connection in public—made the whole night sparkly and unique.

Even then I knew it had nothing to do with Kyle and everything to do with the fact that someone wanted to claim me too, wanted to hold my hand as we looked out at the dark together.

Friday nights at the carnival, with the smell of funnel cakes and the constant whir of rides and games, always take me right back to that hope.

Sitting on my couch at 4:57 p.m. on the Friday of the haunted carnival weekend, waiting to begin a Halloween movie marathon with my parents, does not have the same excitement. While this is the most benevolent grounding of all time since my parents are making me stay home so we can hang out and spend more time together, there's so much pent-up longing inside me for all I'm missing—my last haunted carnival night as a Fableview student.

"I just got off the phone with Kathy Holtzenberg, who is beyond ecstatic to get the chance to fill in for us at the carnival this weekend," Mom says, settling down beside me on the couch with a bowl of popcorn.

Dad's already gotten out his candy stash, and he's halfway into biting through his second sour straw when he responds with "You made it clear it's a onetime thing, right?"

"Yes. I told her we needed some family time, just the three of us. She'll swing by in a little bit to pick up our ghost costumes."

"You really didn't have to do that," I tell them both. It's a little awkward between us. I still feel hurt over how they've thrust everything upon me. But even I can recognize what a big deal it is that they've punted a task over to the Holtzenberg family.

Mom sticks the bowl of popcorn my way, knowing I like to have the first handful. "The haunted carnival is one of the easiest events of the entire season. It's not a big deal to have Kathy and Kevin do it."

Except it *is* a big deal. I wouldn't be surprised if someone brings it up at the final planning committee meeting. *Is everything okay with the Kellers? They let the Holtzenbergs do the carnival weekend.*

"We'd rather be here with you," Dad says, offering me a sour straw.

We've sat this way on our couch countless times in my life—Mom with her right elbow on the arm of the couch, Dad with his feet crisscrossed atop the coffee table. Me in the middle, hands squeezed between my legs, the only one of us who can stay awake for the duration of literally anything we watch.

Mom starts the movie, one we've all seen so many times, we can quote it. Still, we watch in silence, pretending to pay close attention. My parents want something more from this—I'm grounded, after all—but they're not going for it right away. They're buttering me up with popcorn and treats and our favorite Halloween movies first.

"Can we just talk about it?" I blurt. "The anticipation is too much."

Mom presses pause on the remote. "Talk about what, sweetie?" It only takes one look from me to get her to change tactics. "We wanted to have a nice evening with you first."

"Before I sign the paperwork that transfers the title to Pam's Paints over to me, complete with a name change to Darcy's Dabbles or something," I say.

That one gets a chuckle out of Dad.

"Before we tell you that you're right," my mom says, serious.

"I'm . . . right?"

"Yes. We've been perhaps a little too present in your life. We just . . . We love you." At once, she begins to cry, and it's so quick and unexpected that it startles her as much as it does me.

"Oh, Mom," I say, wrapping her in my arms. For as sentimental as she is, she doesn't cry much. "I know you do. I love you too."

"I think . . . we hoped . . . you'd be . . . like us," she says through sniffles.

"Fableview lifers," my dad interjects.

"Neither of us ever wanted to leave here," Mom adds.

Dad nods emphatically. "Never. We've loved it ever since we were younger than you. And we wanted a kid so badly. You know that. It took us a very long time to get you, and once we did, I guess we expected you to pop out liking all the same things we do."

"We figured, if we showed you everything there was to love about this place, you'd never want to leave us."

"I *do* want some of it," I say. It's important that I don't let my sympathy turn into guilt. Their desires for me can be different from mine, and I don't have to feel bad about that. "And maybe someday, I could even want all of it. But I also want a chance to know for sure."

Mom's still fighting hard to return to her dignity, one hand covering her eyes as if that might make the tears stop. "We should have asked you. Which seems very obvious now. But you know, for as old as we are, we're still new to this whole *being a parent to an adult* gig."

I've certainly felt like an adult more times than I can count, but I've never been called an adult before. It's technically not even true yet, since I'm still seventeen, but it's meaningful to have her say it—to recognize I am more than just her precious baby girl.

"Does this mean I'm not grounded anymore?" I try.

"It's not *that* easy," Mom says, letting out a laugh.

"Does it mean that I get to apply to more colleges out of state?" I try next, poking her in the rib. Even if I'm not making any real headway, I'm at least making her smile.

It's Dad who laughs this time. "If I remember correctly, you informed us you'd already done that."

"I applied to *one*," I admit, feeling guilty. "But I do have others I want to look at . . ."

Mom stands up, heading down the hallway toward her room. When she returns, she's holding her laptop. She hands it over to me. "Show us. Tell us what you like about them."

"I don't know what I want to major in or even what exactly I'm looking for from a school," I say as a preface, feeling strangely self-conscious as I place the laptop on our coffee table.

My parents don't give me a hard time for not having a clear vision. They help me imagine a plan in more specific terms instead. For being Fableview lifers, they're very good at knowing what I should look for. Probably because they're good at knowing *me*.

In these last few weeks, it's felt like they haven't really seen me changing, like I've been sending up all these flares, and most have gone right over their heads. But even with all the details they've missed, they still know my interests—the constants that have always been around. We all agree I should find a school that supports my passions, which boil down to art, music, and language. It seems obvious once we've settled on them, but it was something I couldn't yet see, too distracted by my need to prove to them that I should be able to do this at all.

Our evening of movies becomes an evening of research, which wouldn't normally be appealing, but it reminds me of our best past moments, like the time I came home sheepish, admitting to them that, *whoops*, I had an entire rainforest habitat diorama due tomorrow, and I'd forgotten to start it. After a little bit of frustration—and more than one comment about how I should've told them sooner—we gathered up supplies from the art shop and started building, using glue and markers and Popsicle sticks and construction paper, winging it until we came up with a pretty impressive re-creation of the rainforest.

*These* are the parents I love the most. The ones who work with me, who help me when I can't do it alone. Who find the answers I didn't even know I was looking for. Who make something logical out of my mess.

By the time Kathy Holtzenberg has stopped by downstairs to pick up the costumes, we've whittled down my choices to four other schools, and we all seem genuinely excited by the picks, even Mom, who has always had the hardest time with all this. I think about how she inherited the art shop from *her* mom. She's probably had this whole image in her head of the day she'd pass it down to me.

When she returns from giving Kathy Holtzenberg the costumes, I feel such a swell of affection that I hug her again. "Thank you," I say.

"You're still grounded for now," she says from the depths of my squeeze.

"That's not why I'm hugging you. I know this is hard for you. And I really appreciate the fact that you're still letting me try."

Without meaning to, I've started up her tears again. She grabs me back with a newfound urgency. "You can still go to the Fall Ball," she whispers into my hair.

"Really?"

"*Really*. If you want to go, that is," she adds. "No pressure."

"Mom, I still love all our town's traditions," I assure her, tilting my head up to see her. "I just think we should be able to, you know, change up our costumes every once in a while."

"Don't tell me you mean *Ghostbusters* and *Grease*?" she asks, aghast.

"I mean *Ghostbusters* and *Grease*," I say.

With a little more back-and-forth, my dad throwing his hat in the ring for this discussion, they both agree to take the note, promising to look for new costumes with me—*after* Halloween is over.

"So we can get the best deals," Dad says with a wink.

We've gotten so much accomplished that we've all forgotten about the movie. It's me who suggests we commit to finishing it.

Mom presses play, and we make it no more than a minute before Dad claps his hands on his legs and says, "We've gotten everything else out in the open; why don't you go ahead and tell us more about what's going on with Anya?"

"*Ew*," I say involuntarily, chucking a piece of cold popcorn at him.

He puts his hands up. "Hey now, I'm just doing my dad duty."

"Honestly, we're relieved you're not still trying to hang out with Kyle Holtzenberg," Mom whispers, as if Kathy might have followed her up the stairs.

"You guys are the ones letting the Holtzenbergs do the carnival," I remind them, pivoting us away from talk of Anya. Not because I wouldn't tell them. This night of grounding has been unexpectedly nice. But there are still so many complicated feelings swirling around in my head and my heart. Talking about it with my parents before I talk about it with Anya doesn't sit right.

"We shouldn't have done that," Mom agrees. "But we wanted you to know we're serious about being here for you. And it's too late now to stop Kathy. She's probably driving seventy down the boulevard, laughing the whole way."

When we finally continue the movie, Mom and Dad make it about thirty minutes before they're asleep.

I could say I'd rather be at the carnival, but this moment is so sweet, so typical yet so endearing, that I really am glad they've grounded me. Because now that I'm officially allowed to apply for colleges, I know for certain that I'll be leaving them soon.

Next October, I'll be living in a dorm on a campus somewhere far from here. There will be no Halloween movie marathons with me wedged between them as they snooze.

So for now, I'm exactly where I want to be.

# 26

# ANYA

We walk between stalks of corn higher than our heads. Grace swears this winding dirt path will lead us where we need to go, but the inky night provides little assistance. It's hard not to get spooked by the way the corn rustles and sways in random, unpredictable intervals, no connection to the wind or anything we can see.

I expect Grace to be skittish too, but she's hard-eyed and ready, hands tucked under the gigantic backpack she's put on for the occasion. She's dressed in all black. No costume in sight. *The most serious person in the world*, I think.

She pulls a walkie-talkie out of a side pocket and hands it to me, then takes out another and talks into it. "Doyle, this is Manalo, over and out."

"We're standing side by side."

"Doyle. Please. Whimsy," she says, still using the walkie. "Don't ruin this with your cynicism."

I lift the walkie-talkie to my mouth. "It scares me that you're starting to make sense."

"There's nothing worse than robbing yourself of joy because you think you need to be seen as unaffected."

Feeling brave or maybe even playful, I set the walkie-talkie on the ground to take a lunging step forward, bringing my arms up straight into the air, my shoulders pressed against my ears. "How's *this* for joyful?"

I attempt my first cartwheel in years. Blood rushes through me like a glitter-fueled rain stick, sloshing back and forth. When I try to land, my feet aren't quite ready for the ground. I end up flopping onto my butt, the dry earth providing me no cushion.

"Excellent," Grace says, still determined—treating this like a full-scale mission—but also impressed. "I didn't know you had that in you."

I catch myself smiling, a little bit proud of myself in spite of the failed landing. "One of my older cousins made me learn basic tumbling when I lived with her."

"For, like, magical reasons?"

"No. She just wanted someone to watch her do flips all day, and I was the one who was around."

"Nice. By the way, I have some minor bad news," Grace says.

I brush the dirt off my butt and pick up my walkie. "You let me do a cartwheel before you told me there's bad news?"

"I'd do it again if you wanted to try a handstand."

I stare at her.

"It's been a while since I've seen one of those particular glares. *Memories.*"

"Please tell me the bad news."

"Darcy's grounded," she says.

Grace continues walking, and I have no choice but to follow. "Why are we in the middle of a cornfield on our way to the secret back entrance of this carnival if she's not going to see what we do?"

"Patience, Doyle. Please."

The cornstalks finally flatten out, and we come up against a fence. Beyond it are huge overhead lights, like the kind they use at football games, illuminating the clearing. We can't see much from where we are, facing the back of what looks to be a funhouse maze, but we can hear the faint hum of waltzing carnival music. Grace continues leading me around the fence, weaving us in and out of the corn like we're dodging invisible lasers.

"Why do you know how to do this?" I ask her. When she doesn't answer, I take out the walkie and try again. "Manalo, this is Doyle. Paging you for an explanation."

"Parker showed me last year," she walkies back. "They didn't want to pay the entrance fee."

"The famed Parker Holt. A rebel. Will I ever meet them?"

"*Maybe*," Grace says, but not into the walkie. She looks back to tell me, and it's small but somehow significant.

We reach a corner of the fence with a gap wide enough to walk through it sideways. Grace gives me another look, making sure I'm appreciating how well she's navigated us to this point. She tosses her backpack in first, then we step through, weaving in and out of the crowd until we reach a large tent with a ramshackle wooden sign at the opening—the words HAUNTED HOUSE sprayed atop it in ominous red paint. There are red handprints smeared across the tent, and a special effect smoke puffing around the entrance.

"It already looks pretty cool," I admit. From the way Grace

and Darcy spoke about this, I expected to find something cutesier. But this is sufficiently creepy, if not particularly detailed. It's visibly a tent, not a house, for one. But all in all, it's still effective, especially set against the cornstalks.

"Yeah, and then you get inside, and the Kellers are covered in bedsheets pretending to be a married ghost couple, and they follow you around for a few rooms saying 'Boo,' and it gets a little less appealing," Grace says. "Though they've decided to ground themselves with Darcy. So Mr. and Mrs. Holtzenberg are filling in."

"Kyle's parents are running this?" I've learned enough Fableview town history to process how significant this is. Monumental, really.

Grace smiles. "See? You *do* understand why we couldn't cancel."

"Our mission isn't to make this better anymore, is it?" I ask. "We'll be making it worse?"

"Doyle, you *are* a little sinister, after all," she says with a grin. "No, we're still going to make it better. But if the town doesn't like it, they'll think it's the Holtzenbergs' fault, and we'll keep our identities disguised. If they do like it, we can come forward as the creators. Or we can just bask in the private glory of knowing we've made a sufficiently scary upgrade to the haunted house. Either way, we're safe to really go for it."

All this way and we haven't discussed the plan. When Grace doesn't move, I suspect she doesn't actually have one. She's figured me, plus magic, plus this tent would somehow alchemize into a functioning setup.

There are about a dozen things I could tell her that would let her down in this moment. I could use my magic to patch up the hole at the edge of the tent, tattered from years of wear. That's not the kind of power that's going to shake up this town. But Grace has gone through all this trouble to help me without anything for her to gain from it. She has no motive outside of wanting Darcy to be happy. And, I guess, wanting me to be happy. So I don't tell her all the things I can't do.

Instead I look at her with a smile and say into my walkie, "Manalo, it's time to begin our first run-through of the haunted house. Copy that?"

"Copy that," she says.

We walk into the tent.

# 27

# DARCY

If my parents didn't want me to sneak out every once in a while, they wouldn't have given me the bedroom with the balcony. This used to be my mom's room when she lived here with my grandparents, and I know for certain she did her fair share of dashing off into the night, because the first time I ever tried it myself, there were obvious spaces for my hands and feet to go, ledges and jutting rocks placed in the exact spots you'd need when making your way to the ground. Which is why, even after our sentimental evening of bonding, I don't feel bad about doing this. If anything, it's another proud tradition I'm carrying on— a continuation of my mother's legacy.

And frankly, I'm not missing my last Friday at the haunted carnival.

I have no transportation other than my old bike, chained up to a rack at the end of our alley. It's been so long since I've ridden it that it no longer stands on its own. It's dusty and dirt-covered from spending countless undignified months on its side. The tires are so low on air that they're squishy to the touch.

"Please," I say, like the bike is sentient. In this town, maybe it is. "Just one ride. That's all I need."

I'm not even off the cobblestones of Fableview Boulevard when the back tire blows out. It's as loud as a firework and just as shocking. I panic, worried one of my neighbors is going to come out and see me, and my gentle grounding will become something much more intense.

A car drives down the boulevard, and it's all I can do to stay looking forward as I wheel my bike beside me, hoping it's not someone I know. Perhaps a tourist has come through to enjoy the twinkle lights.

"Darce?" Of course it's not a tourist—it's Kyle Holtzenberg, who is developing a supernatural talent for always being everywhere I don't want him to be.

"Hey, Kyle," I say, not making eye contact, wheeling my bike forward.

He's driving two miles an hour with his head leaned out of his rolled-down window. "You goin' to the carnival? My parents made me come back home to pick up a basket for them. Something they swear they need. I was like, 'Mom, you can't be serious.' But she was deadass. I was in the middle of a legendary basketball game. People were gathering around me. I made something like one hundred or two hundred baskets in a row."

"That's a wide estimate," I interject.

"Yeah, well, they cut me off to come do this. I had to let go of the exact stats, or it'd eat me up inside. Anyway, I feel like I'm living your life right now. The errand boy."

"Yep."

"I can give you a ride," he says. "Since we're headed the same way."

"No need. I can walk just fine."

"Is this about Anya?"

This gets me to change directions. I don't know what my plan is, but I'll cut across the creek and swim if needed. Anything to avoid this conversation.

Kyle puts his car in reverse.

"C'mon," I plead. "I don't want to talk to you about her. Not when you're the one who told her that you and I are 'kind of dating.'" I say the last part in his tone of voice, an impression so mocking that it teeters on the edge of being mean-spirited.

He parks his car in the middle of the street and gets out. It would seem imposing, maybe even scary, if he wasn't looking at me with such surprising . . . kindness?

"I shouldn't have said that," he admits. When he moves, it's not to reach for me but to grab my bike so he can be the one to wheel it along.

"You don't even know where I'm going," I say.

"Neither do you."

*Touché.*

"I could tell that she liked you," he says, bringing the conversation back to Anya. "And you liked her. And, you know, I can admit that I got a little threatened at first, all right? I know that's not cool to say, but it's true. That's why I called her your girlfriend at the orchard. I want you to know I'm okay with it now. I'm *not* okay with her taking my apple bobbing prize, though. That five hundred dollars was for my Lego castle."

"Lego castle?"

Kyle does a flailing movement with his hands, like he's only just now realized what he said and he knows there's no way to take it back. "My little brother is obsessed with them. We have the medieval town square already, and he really wants to add the castle."

"It costs five hundred dollars?"

"Basically. They're super expensive. But they're really cool. Very detailed. You can do all kinds of stuff with them."

"Like be a charming prince?" I tease.

"Yeah," he says with a grin. "Exactly."

I can't tell if Kyle would really spend that much money on making his little brother happy, or if he's lying and it's actually for himself. Either way, it's sweet. Kyle's just so Kyle, I never once thought about how he bonds with his brother. It's a good reminder that even when you think you've got a person all figured out, they might still have some surprises up their sleeve.

"I'm sorry you didn't win. And that you're on errand duty. I really do get how much that sucks," I tell him.

"It's fine. Anya better take you out on a nice date with all that cash." Someone honks at Kyle's parked car, and both of us turn. "Are you sure you don't need a ride?"

"Actually, yeah," I say. "I do."

We leave my bike against the last shop on the boulevard, and I hop into Kyle's car.

"You really like her, huh, if you're breaking your whole Fableview rule?" he asks.

"I do," I admit.

"Nice," he says. "She's kind of intense, though."

I give him a warning look, and he lifts his hands from the steering wheel for a moment. "Hey, hey. It's not a problem. Just a fact."

"She is," I tell him, softening.

"Did she tell you she almost failed gym class last year?" he asks.

"I'm sure that was your fault."

He seems to really think on this before he says, "Damn. Maybe it was. Anyway, seems like she kind of makes you braver."

I'm ready to make another argument, but in his weirdly sage Kyle way, he's right again. She *does* make me braver. Even this act, sneaking out to see her. All the changes I've made since that night she first showed up at the art shop. She's been the one encouraging me when everyone else has been reminding me over and over of the risks. The consequences. The ways it could all go wrong. She's always pushed me toward the good.

I ask Kyle more questions about his Lego collection, learning he and his little brother, Karl—the Holtzenbergs are very committed to the *K*-name theme—have built up quite the dynasty.

As he tells me about all the sets they've built together over the years, and the reasons they picked each one, I realize this is probably the most earnest conversation Kyle and I have ever had. He says random things a lot, but he's a good guy. There's surely a girl out there for him who can appreciate his muscles *and* his mind. He can be someone else's charming prince.

It's nice to have him finally recognize that girl will never be me.

"Anya and I aren't really talking right now," I say.

For whatever reason, it's easier to confide in Kyle than it is my parents. He knows me in such a different light. Even though his parents want my family's empire, Kyle just wants to be Kyle. He has never seemed to care that dating me could grant him access to the keys to our Halloween kingdom. He is so exquisite in his simplicity sometimes that I find myself actually wanting to know his take on this situation.

"What did she do?" he asks.

"It's my fault too," I say quickly. "I didn't listen to her when she told me something about herself. And when that turned out to be true, I realized that she had this whole plan for me that she hadn't asked about."

"Is it about her being a witch?" he asks. I turn my head to him, trying to see if he's kidding. "I mean, isn't her whole family?" he follows up, another lifting of his hands from the wheel, forever playing defense.

Ignoring this is my only solution. It's not the point anyway. What matters is that we didn't talk about her plans for me in her initiation.

"Okay, sorry, yeah," Kyle says, reading my silence as anger. "I know we're, like, not supposed to bring up the actual magic here. Right?"

"I guess," I say weakly.

After another bout of silence, he says, "Maybe that's why she did it. Made a plan without asking. Because she knew it's all this big secret thing already, and she was stressed about whatever plan she'd made for you. Don't we all kind of do that when we're stressed? Tell ourselves lies to get through it or sometimes lies that make it worse, you know?"

Never in my life would I have expected this conversation to

be so revelatory. I've been heading to the carnival for a lot of reasons—tradition, enjoyment. And, yeah, maybe to see Anya and figure this whole thing out between us.

Now I feel this need to apologize too. Like when she had the cut on her hand, I want to be the one who makes sure she's okay.

"Kyle, it's time to floor it."

# 28

# ANYA

The haunted house looks like a night at Aunt Cal's after she's turned off most of the lights. Dark and a little strange, but not very frightening. There are the famed bedsheet ghosts, who chase you through the first three rooms. There is a fake clown dummy that pops out of a closet at what Grace estimates to be seventeen-second intervals. She has a very strong internal clock.

There's a motion-censor skeleton that sits up in bed and lets out a moan of agony when you pass. Some ominous noises playing on a loop. And another fog machine again at the very end, carrying the weight of the world on its cloudy back before returning you to the rest of the carnival.

Grace *does* have a plan. It's wild and way too ambitious, asking more of me than just my magic. But it exists, and it could be a good one, if we can pull it off. Very heavy emphasis on *if*.

To get the lay of the land, we go through the haunted house four more times.

Our last round catches the Holtzenbergs' attention, Kyle's

mom whispering to Grace, "Is everything okay?" like we might be here doing a quality control check on behalf of the Fableview Fall Planning Committee.

That's when we decide it's time to move into phase two.

Grace has packed a lot of stuff in her backpack. At first glance, it all seems random and excessive. She has four flashlights that she's covered in blue gel sheets. A bunch of plants, from flowers to succulents to vines, all in various states of distress. A bag of fake blood. Two costumes that look like cheap Victorian gowns. Random accessories, like necklaces, rings, and wigs. A rubber snake.

"Sorry," Grace says, holding the snake. "That's not for this."

Hidden in the shadows behind the tent, we change our clothes, pulling the scratchy polyester dresses over our heads.

"I've never seen you in yellow before," Grace says.

"Memorize it," I tell her. "Because it will never happen again."

Grace smears fake blood onto my face. I drag bloody hand-prints across her dress.

We practice our plan as best we can. It's very hard with the limited space we have, not to mention the lack of an audience. The only way to really know if we will be successful is to try it when it counts.

We've memorized the haunted house's layout, and we make our way to the side with the skeleton bedroom. There's a tear at the bottom of the tent, not unlike several others I've noticed on our walk-throughs.

Closing my eyes, putting my hand on the small tear, I let every stress and worry of the past month bear down on me. Instead of mending together, the tough, sturdy fabric of the tent begins ripping apart, a jagged opening stretching upward until it's tall enough for us to pass through.

Grace pats me on the back. "That was *cool*."

Even though it's a silly gesture, it does make me feel a little proud of myself. There is something freeing about exploring this other side of my magic. None of my lessons have ever focused on breaking things instead of fixing them.

Inside the tent, we set up as fast as possible, then crouch in the corner of the bedroom.

"Are you ready?" I whisper to Grace, hearing the soft rumbles of laughter and screams from a group in the distance.

"I'm nervous," she says back. It's the first sign of weakness she's shown since we started this, and even in the low light of this tent's fake bedroom, I can spot an unfamiliar worry in her eyes.

A plan is different when it's in the talking stage. Everything seems exciting. Daring. Now the reality is here, and what we're attempting is bold. Dramatic. And risky.

The incoming group is only a room away, letting out fake high-pitched shrieks for the clown dummy, then laughing at each other. They sound like high school students, and it spikes my adrenaline to an all-time high. Our first audience will be a group of teenage boys.

The bedroom door creaks open, and Grace doesn't move into position. We can't *both* be nervous. We can't both second-guess ourselves.

"C'mon," I whisper. "Let's show the world your dark, gothic soul."

It's quick, but it's enough. Grace goes to her designated spot.

Our skeleton friend does his part first, sitting up in bed, prompting another round of fake screams from the boys.

Grace seizes my wrist. She yells, in something sort of like a British accent but not *quite*, "No, please, no!" while thrashing on the ground.

I assume my position, looming behind her. I have the vines in my hand, and I bring them over her head until they land in front of her neck. We've got the flashlights positioned on us to make sure everything is bright enough to see. The blue gels make it look appropriately moody.

I pretend to choke Grace with the vines. We're dressed kind of old-timey, like we're from the 1800s, but if a teen soap opera with a limited budget and no fear of historical inaccuracy dressed us. It might matter to someone, but if Grace has taught me anything, it's that commitment is all that's required to pull off a unique ensemble.

"*Lady Marbles*," Grace cries, still using her quasi-British accent. "Release me at once."

"Never!" I pull the vines tighter, knowing Grace's hands on them are preventing me from doing any actual harm. The boys are watching us silently, not yet sure what to make of this spectacle. The pressure of their judgment heightens my nerves. That would be a bad thing under any other circumstance. Right now, for what I need to do next, it's exactly right.

Grace is faced out toward them, her back pressed into mine, the vines against her throat as she makes coughing, choking sounds. "Please," she begs, her voice hoarse.

Squeezing my eyes shut, I picture the hot breath of the worst summer day, a sticky July afternoon that would smother out any plant unlucky enough to be in direct sunlight. I picture every unkind thought these boys are probably having about how silly and immature this whole thing is.

Magic pulses through me—that wiry, jagged feeling I get when I have too much of it, pooling in my hands like how sweat builds when I'm nervous.

The vines begin to *crackle*. Spark.

For a moment, they're actually on fire.

When Grace startles, it severs my connection to my magic, and the fire snuffs out immediately. The vines turn to dust, as we initially planned, crumbling into nothing.

Grace looks at me with genuine malice. She's still in this, all the way committed. The way we've staged it, she looks like the one who magically destroyed the vines, breaking free of my hold. She said this would be her *Carrie* moment, covered in blood and out for revenge. She wanted it to come off like she's snapped, like whatever my character has done is bringing out some unexplained power in her.

She plays it perfectly, her desire to get me back so believable that it isn't difficult for me to rise, lunging at the guests in the room like they might be my next target instead. I chase them out of the skeleton room and into the final hallway before the exit.

This time their screams are real.

Grace pretends to pull me back—to catch me.

"Run!" she tells the guests. "Save yourselves!"

And they do. They run like they're truly scared I might do something to them. Or Grace might.

When we return to the skeleton room, we're both still so in it that we don't say anything at all. We're standing side by side, breathing hard, in utter disbelief.

The skeleton rises from his bed to greet us.

We laugh. Only a little. Low and proud.

"It really worked," I whisper.

"That was *amazing*," Grace says. "They were actually scared. I can't believe the vines caught on fire. It looked so cool. That was Matt Bautista, Isaac Diaz, and some other guys I didn't recognize."

I didn't know any of them, but Grace goes on to tell me about their reactions in more detail as we set up our act again, waiting for the next group to come through. Apparently, Matt had tears in his eyes at one point. Isaac was holding on to his jeans when he ran out, like something had happened.

Grace pats my back again. "They completely believed it."

We hear the next group approaching, and we hurry into position. I find myself even more committed, certain now that this will work. The fire doesn't catch again, but the effect is still cool when the plants turn to dust.

It's the most rigorous magic practice I've had in a long time, and I know with certainty that it's also the most consistent magic I've ever done, the same way I know when food tastes particularly good or when music is well written. It's a soul-deep satisfaction that makes me wish there was a Doyle here to see me.

*I don't want to give this up*, I realize.

This power makes me who I am. And I like it about myself.

The groups start coming through closer together. At one point, the entire bedroom is packed with people, and I don't even have to chase them out. They start running when the vines disintegrate, the youngest kid among them screaming with genuine terror.

It's such an adrenaline high that I don't even notice the Holtzenbergs enter. Not until Grace is tugging on my hand, whispering my name over and over. Both of Kyle's parents are struggling to get their ghost costumes off their heads to see us in full.

"*Go*," I whisper, shoving Grace toward the hole in the tent. She thinks I'm following right behind her, but once she's through, I mend the tear in the tent.

It's only me who will take the fall.

The Holtzenbergs get free of their bedsheet costumes right as I finish patching up the hole. I've been practicing magic so much that I don't even have to think hard to do it. I'm already centered, already steady. The rest of the Doyles really should see this. They would be amazed at how one night in this haunted house has done more for my training than several years in their homes.

Maybe it would be enough to let me into the coven without a protector. Maybe I'm the one who could teach *them* a thing or two.

"Excuse me," Mrs. Holtzenberg says. When I turn to face her, she screams. Probably because I'm covered in blood and wearing a weird gown inside this haunted house that's only ever had two bedsheet ghosts and some old animatronics.

"I'm not a real killer," I tell her for some reason. This doesn't make it any better.

"Kevin!" she shouts.

Her husband grabs my arm like I'm the kind of trouble that needs apprehending. Which I guess I sort of am. He drags me toward the back of the haunted house.

"We're taking you to the *tent*," he says, like I know what that means. We're already in a tent.

I don't bother to resist. The only time I even lift my head is when we get back outside, and I catch sight of Grace along the edge of the fence. She starts forward like she's going to sacrifice herself too, and I shake my head. She's not going down with me.

Turns out that the tent is some sort of makeshift security center. There's one older man in here, not a cop but an employee of some security firm, wearing their logo on his ill-fitting polo as he eats a hot dog while watching a fuzzy livestream of various corners of the carnival on an iPad. He can't be watching very closely, since Grace and I snuck in without notice.

His jaw drops when he sees me. I remember that I'm covered in blood, dressed like some kind of low-rent Lizzie Borden. With Mr. Holtzenberg holding me as if I'm dangerous, it seems like I've committed a real crime—the kind this guy is probably not at all equipped to handle.

"She was causing a *scene* in the haunted house," Mrs. Holtzenberg explains. "Chasing people out. They were screaming in horror."

The man scrambles to wipe mustard off the corner of his mouth. "Is anyone hurt?" he asks, fumbling with the crumbs that have dropped onto his folding-table desk.

"No," Mrs. Holtzenberg says. "Just our business."

If this wasn't so serious, I could almost laugh. Grace and I were able to go through the haunted house four times in a row without interruption; that's how slow the business was. By the time we'd finished our last performance, the place was packed.

"Why did you do it?" the security guard asks me.

I'm trying to come up with a reason that's safe enough to share but also sounds compelling.

*I really love Halloween, and I think you guys don't do it in an interesting way.*

Sounds weird.

*I'm passionate about haunted houses having genuine scares.*

Also weird.

*The person I like really wanted this to be a cooler thing than it is, and I took it upon myself to make that happen so that she's hopefully impressed when she hears about it at some undetermined later date.*

I don't have to answer, because Kyle Holtzenberg himself bursts into the tent. "I put her up to it," he declares.

The *"What?"* that flies out of my mouth is involuntary. Unstoppable. In what world is Kyle Holtzenberg trying to take the fall for me?

"This was all my idea," he tells his parents. "I dared her to do this."

"Kyle Kristopher Holtzenberg. Why on earth would you do that?" Mrs. Holtzenberg asks. She's got that edge to her voice that I recognize from movies—a parent who has *had enough.*

"I was trying to win Darcy back," he says, and now I'm twisted all the way around in my chair, in the front row for this riveting piece of theater. "I know this is usually her parents' thing, and she was so upset about seeing them lose it. I thought that if I made sure it was a disaster, she'd maybe go to the Fall Ball with me after all."

The Holtzenbergs have their ghost costumes draped over their arms, and Mrs. Holtzenberg sets hers on the security guard's desk. "Kyle, sweetie," she says, putting both hands on either side of his face. "You have got to be serious."

For a moment, I think she knows he's lying. Because *obviously* he's lying. His story is ridiculous, and she wants him to tell the truth. But, no, she's bought the whole thing so completely that she means Kyle needs to shape up his life. She's saying he needs to be serious about himself. About his decisions.

It's Mr. Holtzenberg who still has doubts. He puts a hand on me, pulling the attention back to me after Kyle's stolen the show. "He really asked you to do this?"

"I did," Kyle answers before I can. He widens his eyes as much as possible, a face that says, *Don't you dare say it isn't true.*

I do something that might pass for a nod but is really more like a stiffening of my neck, and the security guard says, "Well then, what would you like me to do?"

"Let her go," Kyle says. "Cuff me instead."

"No one's getting handcuffed," the security guard informs us. He looks to the Holtzenbergs almost like he's asking their permission for the next part. "But I can keep him supervised in the tent until the end of the night?"

"That won't be necessary," Mrs. Holtzenberg tells him, gathering up her ghost costume again.

*If both Holtzenberg parents are here, who is supervising the haunted house?* I wonder. Not that it matters. But somehow, I know the Kellers would never have let this happen this way. Then again, Kyle's dramatic and unexpected defense of me wouldn't have worked on them. There's no sense in imagining that reality, because the one I'm in is the one where I'm free.

The Holtzenbergs leave first, telling Kyle they'll discuss this again at the end of the night.

"You're in big trouble," Mrs. Holtzenberg says as a final threat, pulling the bedsheet back over her head, leaving me alone with Kyle.

"You owe me five hundred dollars," Kyle tells me once we've exited the tent afterward, back in the land of funnel cakes and Ferris wheels.

"Is *that* why you did this? Because I'll go back in there and tell them the truth." I turn toward the tent.

"Hold on," Kyle says. "I was just saying, you know, if you felt the need to pay me for my kindness, that amount would do it . . ."

"Kyle, I have no idea why you just barged into that tent and told your parents an elaborate lie on my behalf, but I do know that I feel no need to give you my apple bobbing contest earnings. You don't know how tense the final was. You weren't there. I was bobbing for my life."

"Fine," he says, having the audacity to sound annoyed about it.

Our walk has synced, and it jars me so much to notice it that I wonder if I should go find Grace and explain to her what happened. But somehow, I feel compelled to see this through, despite Kyle's commitment to pestering me in the aftermath. He's still annoying, but it's the kind of annoying I've grown to appreciate.

I'm about to say as much when I hear her.

"It *was* you," she says.

Julia is here, because of course she is. All my good feelings fly out the window at the sight of her. "You used your magic in the haunted house," she says. "We saw you." Her boyfriend stands behind her with his arms crossed. "I thought you couldn't use your magic for other people. Or was that just another one of your lies?"

"I never lied to you," I say.

"She's a *witch*," she says to Kyle.

"Yeah," he says. "I know."

"But do you *really* know? That she has the power to bring people back to life, and she just doesn't use it?"

For the first time, I really see her. Beneath the anger and the accusations, there is hurt. She didn't want to lose her grandfather, and she needed someone to blame for it. That someone was me. No matter what I do, I will never be able to change that.

"Julia, I'm sorry I couldn't save your grandfather." My apology isn't about my powers. It's about life itself. Sometimes it's cruel. Sometimes it takes the things you love from you and you don't have any say in the matter. That's what I'm sorry about.

Her face flushes as red as her hair. "I don't want your apology. I want everyone to know the truth about you."

"They already know," I tell her, for once feeling ready to meet this moment. "And they don't care. So now what? You follow me everywhere I go? You move here and announce to every person who comes through town that I'm a witch? In Fableview? A town that celebrates Halloween for an entire month? Which is the whole reason you came here in the first place?"

"Kinda seems to me like you might be obsessed with her," Kyle interjects.

I could hug him.

I really, really could.

"Nobody in our town will care what you have to say," he continues. He's on a real hot streak now, and he knows it, his voice getting louder and more confident with every word. "We will all choose Anya over you. So maybe get over it. Or just leave. You won't be missed."

The strangest thing happens. Tears spring to my eyes. Over

Kyle Holtzenberg. He's defended me so well that Julia and her boyfriend actually walk away.

"Damn. She sucks. How do you even know her?" he asks once she's gone. He looks down, realizes I'm crying, and gets startled. "Was I not supposed to do that? I was kinda just following your vibe."

"No, no. That was amazing. I'm just . . ." I can't believe I'm about to say this to Kyle Holtzenberg. "It means a lot that you stuck up for me."

"Oh." He smiles, proud of himself. "Yeah. I guess I did. That was nice of me."

"It was."

"I'm a pretty good dude."

"You are."

"Who totally deserves five hundred dollars."

I roll my eyes. "Finish telling me about how your first rescue mission of the night happened."

"Not before I get a funnel cake. All this hero stuff has made me work up an appetite."

What a funny pair we must make—Kyle in a Fableview Basketball shirt, eating a funnel cake, and me in a blood-covered yellow gown beside him, patiently waiting for him to either wipe the sugar off his mouth or tell me the rest of what happened.

He feels the intensity of my stare and clears his throat. "Okay, so when we couldn't find you, we ran into Grace. She told us what happened. And I don't know. I just didn't think you deserved the trouble. I know we kinda bug each other, but really, when you think about it—"

"Hold on," I say. "Who is 'we'?"

"Oh. Me and Darcy. She came here to talk to you." He takes another bite of funnel cake. "Anyway. I was saying that I know we bug each other, but it's kinda like our deal. Right? Like, that's just a bit? Like when you pretended you were in love with me?"

I stop him. Put my hands on his shoulders, not very much unlike how his own mother held his face a few minutes ago. "Kyle," I say, sweet despite my dwindling patience. "Where is Darcy now?"

"Oh yeah. Duh. You probably want to see her."

"Yes," I confirm.

"She's at the Ferris wheel," he tells me.

I take off toward it. A few steps into my jog, I break. "Hey, Kyle," I call out. He's standing exactly where I left him.

"Yeah?"

"Thank you."

His whole face lights up, the biggest, dopiest grin I've ever seen. "It's no problem. Now go get your girl."

# 29

# DARCY

The ride operator is about to bring the bar down over Grace and me when Anya runs up covered in fake blood, wearing a frilly Victorian dress I recognize as one of Grace's Halloween costumes from two years ago. Seeing her here, I know Kyle's plan has worked as he said it would, and I might just owe him five hundred dollars for it. That's a problem for later.

For now, Anya is here. She's okay. And she's wearing yellow. Which is worth quite a lot.

"Hold on," Anya says to the ride operator. "I need to get on."

"Doyle," Grace says, raising her fists to cheer. "*You* are a real one!" This gets a bashful half smile out of Anya, and it fuels Grace to embellish as only she can, telling the story again as if she hasn't already breathlessly relayed it to me three previous times. "She *completely* saved me. Literally sealed me from getting back into the tent."

The ride operator lets out a grunt of frustration.

Grace says, "Sorry, sorry. I'll excuse myself." Climbing out of the seat, she pats Anya on the head. "Seriously, Doyle, you're a legend. That was definitely the best haunted house this carnival has ever seen. The Holtzenbergs don't understand horror like we do. Twin dark souls."

Grace winks, and Anya slides into her seat.

We jolt forward and then jerk back, settling into our spots as the Ferris wheel begins to move again.

"Hi," I say, my voice small.

"*Hi*," Anya says back.

The Ferris wheel juts us out over the carnival. Every piece of this place that's so familiar to me shrinks smaller as we rise, like it can fit into my hand.

"Nice costume," I tell her.

"I figured it was finally time to show some of that Fableview enthusiasm I'm always hearing about."

"Not enough of our looks involve fake blood. As usual, you've found a way to push our boundaries."

Closer to the top, it's so black around the edge of the carnival that it looks limitless, an infinite stretch of nothing. It doesn't matter that I can't really see what's out there. I know it like the back of my hand.

"The creek is over there," I whisper. I take this as an excuse to lean in to Anya. My finger points west, and I rest my other hand on her leg.

"I hear that's where all the kids go to be alone," she replies.

"We're pretty alone up here too," I remind her.

We can see the feet swinging from the cart above us. If we looked behind our seat, we could probably see the cart beneath us. But it doesn't matter. No one can reach us here. That's what counts.

"I'm sorry," she tells me. "I never should have told my parents you would be my protector. Or I should've told you about it much earlier, especially since I never meant for it to be true."

"*I'm* sorry," I insist right back. "I had all this adrenaline from telling my parents about college. I was too in my own head to hear you. I know it's not easy for you, after the way Julia abandoned you."

We're above Fableview now, at the peak of the Ferris wheel. The ride jerks to a stop. Maybe there is someone on the ground, desperate to get on the ride like Anya was with me. Maybe there are other people here with us. But none of them matter.

Not when the two of us are on top of the world together.

"Everything she told you about yourself was a lie," I say. "You are the most thoughtful person I know. You're the only reason I've been able to do half the things I've done this month. I think if I hadn't met you, I wouldn't really know myself the way I do now. I'd still be in this fog, waiting to figure it all out sometime down the road. But thanks to you, I get to know myself more *here*. Now."

I reach for her hand. It's a question. A risk. Will she accept this? Will it be enough?

She grabs on without hesitation, weaving her fingers between mine.

"You don't understand how much you mean to me," she says.

"Yes, I do," I tell her. "Because it's the same way I feel about you too."

When we look out again into the yawning darkness, all my aches float away, off to the clouds, replaced with joy.

"We're dating," I say. It's no longer a teasing question. It's a statement. A fact.

"Hold on." Anya jerks enough that our seat rocks. We both let out tiny yips of surprise. "Sorry." She angles herself inward, knees pressing against my side. "Darcy Keller, will you be my girlfriend?"

"Obviously," I say back. "Will you be mine?"

"Always." She brings our hands to her mouth and kisses mine, sealing us to this.

The ride starts moving again, bringing us backward. Our view is no longer of the carnival but of the ride itself, the rainbow of lights decorating the wheel, and all the carts around us, legs swinging in delight.

"Did you know Piper's a witch too?" I ask.

"What?"

"See!" I say, delighted by her surprise. "That's what I said too! It's not always that obvious, is it?"

"My aunt has dead animals on her mantel," she says.

"I thought she was sentimental."

"Speaking of Piper and my aunt, Cal used to date Piper's dad."

"What?"

"That's what I said too!" Anya teases, mimicking my voice with affection. "He's actually Cal's protector. That's the reason why she doesn't want mine to be a romantic interest. He broke her heart. Cheated on her with another woman."

"That sounds like Mr. Blake," I say. "He did it to Piper's mom too."

"What an asshole."

"Well, seeing as I'm now officially your girlfriend, who do you think could be your protector instead?" She moves to pull her hand away, but I don't let her. She needs to know I'm with her, no matter what. Even through the hard stuff.

"My parents came out here to find one for me," she says. "They knew you were never my real choice. They want to ask Kyle."

This gets a belly laugh from me, rocking our cart again. "I mean, he did just save you from a night in the slammer."

"Yeah, if by 'slammer' you mean a night with an old guy eating a hot dog in a tent," she tells me. "That was nice of him, but he asked me for five hundred dollars for it."

"That little shit," I mutter. "He asked me for that too. Thank god we told each other. He would've made out with a thousand bucks."

"I'd never have paid him. And I wouldn't ask him to be my protector either. Though it was nice of him to take the fall for me. He defended me against Julia too."

"What? She's here?" I ask, looking out as if maybe I can spot her red hair from this height.

"Yeah," she says. "She confronted me a little bit ago. And Kyle actually scared her off."

"Good," I say. "She sucks."

This makes Anya laugh. "She did have some good qualities, but I can't remember them anymore."

"It's okay. I don't need to know her complexities. As your girlfriend, I get to just hate her."

Anya kisses me on the cheek, sending a fluttering thrill through my whole body. "So what happens if you don't have a protector by your birthday?" I ask.

"Then I get kicked out of the coven. They remove my powers, and I'm banished."

"I'm sorry," I say again. "That's horrible. I can see why you did what you did. I wish I could help."

"Yeah, but helping me would mean you aren't my girlfriend." She leans in for another kiss, this time on my mouth.

"That would be a terrible thing," I say, talking with my lips against hers.

"*Terrible*," she echoes. Then she kisses me. Deep and warm and right. My heart could burst into confetti.

We reach the bottom of the ride. The operator lifts the bar to make us exit, despite my request to let us go for one more round.

Grace is waiting for us, grinning. "I took such a cute picture of you two up there," she says, showing us her phone. "God. I'm such a good friend, aren't I?"

I give Anya a look that she doesn't receive. It's crystal clear what she should do. Who she should pick.

But it's not my choice to make. It's hers.

# 4 Days Until Halloween

# 30

# ANYA

Madame Poncik hands a stack of red and green construction paper to the first person in every row, asking them to take a sheet of each and pass the rest back. Darcy sits in front of me, her blond hair soft and flowing, touching the edge of my desk.

My girlfriend.

That will never get old.

When she turns around, she smiles. Her green eyes are the only thing that could ever look this good under the unforgiving fluorescent lights of Fableview High.

"Salut," she says.

"Salut," I respond. "Comment ça va?"

"Très bien." She pretends to struggle with separating the papers, buying us a few more precious seconds. Madame Poncik hates small talk. "Et toi?"

"Comme ci comme ça."

"Just so-so?" she asks in English.

"Oui," I confirm in French. "Je dois regarder l'arrière de la tête de ma copine toute la journée." *I have to look at the back of my girlfriend's head all day.*

"Ah," she says. "Comme c'est triste." *How sad.*

"Do you know what we're doing?" I ask.

"Maybe," she says, turning back around.

I tap her shoulder, leaning in closer. *"Tell me."* My breath tickles her neck, and she shifts in her seat, her shoulder twitching at the feeling.

"Charlotte, Renée," Madame Poncik says, scolding us with our French names.

I sit up straight. I hate getting in trouble.

Once everyone has their papers, Madame Poncik calls Darcy to the front of the class, and I'm wishing I pushed through the fear of being reprimanded a little longer, because Darcy is directly involved in whatever's going on. I track her every movement, telegraphing my confusion. *Look at me. Explain what's going on.*

In a mix of French and English, she tells our class that we will be constructing flowers out of paper today. All my classmates are as confused as I am, but no one is upset by this development. A surprise craft day is on the same level as a surprise movie day, which is to say, it's a very good day indeed. The rest of them don't care to know why we're doing this, only trying to make sure Madame Poncik doesn't change her mind and decide we need to work on our past participles instead.

Darcy demonstrates each step of the process for us. We cut the red construction paper into smaller squares, then fold each sheet until it's as small as the insides of our palms. She shows us how to cut a curve into the paper next. When she unfolds it, she twirls the paper until it's transformed into a petal.

"This is one of the first crafts my parents ever taught me," she tells us. "I was six. And I promise, it's still as cool now as it was back in kindergarten."

"Charlotte! En Français!" Madame Poncik scolds.

"Sorry, sorry," she says, ducking slightly in apology. "Je suis desolée."

It makes me smile to think of six-year-old Darcy at Pam's Paints, doing her best with scissors and glue. She probably learned this on a Monday and started teaching it to Grace by Wednesday, never missing a chance to spread her knowledge or take command of a room.

Patiently, doing her best to use French but mostly getting away with English, she helps our class create flowers. They are red roses with long green stems.

While the project is simple, it's also relaxing. Fun. I can see why Darcy likes art so much. There's a meditative element to it, just you and the medium, working together.

When my rose is nearly constructed, a quick glance around the room tells me some of my classmates haven't done much better than a kindergartener, but everyone is so focused, so serious about their craft, that it's endearing. No one ever lets us do something simple and sweet like this. I don't know if that's Darcy's motivation, but I appreciate it all the same.

Madame Poncik tells Darcy to start wrapping up. Darcy goes around the classroom, collecting the finished roses. I hand mine over without comment, and it's enough to make Darcy's lips quirk. She was expecting me to say something.

It's fun to keep surprising her.

"Charlotte!" Madame Poncik exclaims when Darcy's got everyone's roses collected. "C'est magnifique!" She obviously doubted how effective this craft would be, but she's right to be impressed now.

When Darcy wrangles together all twenty-two roses, tying them together with a little thread of red ribbon, it looks lovely. Not real, but that's not the point. The charm is in the effort.

"Can I do this next part in English?" she asks Madame Poncik.

Madame sighs, narrowing her eyes. Darcy parries with her best please-please-please look. It's enough to make our stern French teacher drop her guard.

"Fine," Madame says, waving dismissively. "Make it count."

Darcy gives her widest, most dazzling grin in return, and my heart does its now-familiar hiccup at the sight.

"I'm sure you're all wondering why you just spent the hour making paper flowers for me," she starts, looking out at our classmates. "Beyond wanting you to experience the satisfaction of a good old-fashioned paper craft and getting to practice my French public speaking, of course." She turns back to Madame Poncik and smiles again.

Madame Poncik nods. "Get on with it, Charlotte."

"I wanted to make my own version of everlasting roses," Darcy says.

A boy named Derek Blankenmeier, one of Kyle's best friends, yells out, "Oui, oui," in his exaggerated French accent, getting everyone to laugh.

"Not now, Derek," Darcy says.

The laughter turns to intrigue, everyone murmuring a version of "What's going on?"

What *is* going on? I wonder too.

"Anya," Darcy says, drawing my attention back. Just hearing

her say my name out loud in front of our class makes a fizzy, bright feeling rise inside me like a shaken soda can. "You've been here long enough to know we have a lot of silly traditions in our town. And one of them is that you're supposed to ask people to the Fall Ball in public. I'm sure you've witnessed it around school. So you might have an idea of what's going on right now."

I'm distantly aware of the way my classmates begin to shift. Heads darting sideways to make eye contact with their friends, understanding dawning over the collective.

Darcy Keller is asking me to the dance. In *public*.

"I used to say I'd never date anyone in Fableview," she says, addressing our classmates like she'd address the painters at her parents' shop or the committee members at the planning meetings. No one is better in front of a crowd than her. Confident and sure, even about this. "And I really believed it."

She shifts her gaze, no longer looking at our classmates.

She's looking at me.

"Until you came along," she says.

Madame Poncik leans back in her computer chair, and the chair lets out a long, loud groan. It's the perfect tension breaker. Everyone laughs.

"Sorry, sorry," she says, whispering. "Keep going."

Darcy takes this chance to walk to my desk, setting the bouquet of flowers atop it. Then she kneels, not on one knee but two, so she's right beside me.

"Anya Doyle, would you go to the Fall Ball with me?"

"Say yes!" Derek calls out, gaining more laughs. Then, like he's expecting trouble from Madame Poncik, he adds, "Say oui!"

It doesn't matter. None of this matters. The whole class could get up and do a dance right now, and I wouldn't care.

"Yes," I tell Darcy, fighting the rise of happy tears. "Of course I will."

I move to hug her, but she doesn't settle for that. She kisses me here, in front of our entire French class. The applause is thunderous, the same as my heart, wild and pounding and joyful.

# 1 Day Until Halloween

# 31

## DARCY

The school gym has been transformed. The whole space is washed in a violet glow, with a black tarp covering the walls usually lined with gym class accomplishments and Fableview sports champions. In front of the tarp are cardboard cutout paintings of iconic locations around town. The shops along the boulevard. The apple orchard. The pumpkin farm. The Fall Ball is the one event of the season that isn't open to just anyone. You need an invite from a local to gain entry. The ball is for all ages, but it tends to be most popular with those of us in high school, though our mayor always attends, as well as some of the most spirited Fableview lifers, like my parents. Even though this is our home, it feels right to dance inside a re-creation of it, like this is our only real chance to celebrate ourselves.

This Fall Ball is the one event where the locals are the tourists.

"My parents and I painted those," I whisper into Anya's ear. She's wearing a long black dress that hugs her body all the way to the floor. Sleek and elegant, just like her, with a black velvet choker around her neck and dark lipstick on her smart mouth.

"They're perfect," she says. "You got the twinkle lights just right."

Somehow she always knows which pieces of art are mine. The lights had taken me weeks to perfect. I obsessed over how much to suffuse them, wanting the street in front of our shop to be perfectly buttery.

"It looks cozy. That's how I know they came from you," she explains, giving me her knowing smirk.

No one's ever described my art as cozy before, but she's right. In everything I create, I'm always looking to capture the comfort of the image. The charm. Even my witch-and-basset-hound painting, which my parents have finally let me teach. I wanted it to have a sense of whimsy but also to capture the safety of Fableview, the gentle hug that is my home.

There are round tables scattered around the dance floor, with a DJ booth up front. Grace waves us over. She's in a dazzling sequined gown that she wouldn't show me beforehand. She told me it was going to be a simple look, and she didn't need to run it by me.

I should have known to expect something jaw-dropping.

Naturally, the disco ball is battling her for the title of the sparkliest thing in the room. She's done her long black hair in waving curls, and there are crystal gems on either side of her face. What she meant is that she doesn't look exaggerated. This isn't a silly Grace Halloween costume or an outlandish, campy ensemble. It's stunning, old-Hollywood-style glamour.

"You look beautiful," I say.

She twirls to give the full effect. Then she holds my hand so I can do the same. I'm in a lavender gown that has enough movement at the bottom to flow outward as I spin, and I would never admit it to Kyle, but I understand what he meant now about wanting to be a charming prince—any charming prince—because this dress makes me feel like a princess, not from any story but my own.

Beside Grace is the one and only Parker Holt. They stretch out a hand to shake mine, which is so formal, so nervously human of them, that I find it endearing. They have on a collared black button-down tucked into black pants, the first few buttons open. Their hair is longer than the last time I saw them, messy in that cool way I've never understood how people achieve.

"Been a while," I say. "How's Scarlet Creek?"

"Same as ever," they say back. "Trying to be Fableview and failing."

Anya steps beside me, and Grace slings an arm around Parker's neck. "Mystery and trouble collide," she says, pointing between Anya and Parker.

Parker gives Grace a kiss on the cheek, and she goes gentle in a way I don't often get to see from her. For all of Parker's faults, they coax out Grace's softer side. I have to appreciate them for that.

Anya introduces herself, going through the usual pleasantries. Then she fixes her face into something serious, pulling Parker closer. "Take good care of her tonight," she whispers.

As we make our way farther into the crowd, almost everyone stops to say hi, complimenting us both on our dresses. They're friendlier to Anya tonight than they've been all year, and I know it's because of the way my Fall Ball ask sent ripples through the school. But she's done so much other work to become the person she is on my arm. If that's what it took to have her finally catch the eye of our classmates, I'd do it again a hundred times over.

Anya takes me by surprise when she presses her body into mine to whisper, "I want to dance."

My eyes light up with hope.

"I don't want to be the person I've been anymore, who's so scared of everything," she continues. "I want to make this night count. And I know that if I'm the one lucky enough to be here with you, then I better get out onto that floor and give you the night you deserve. It might be one of my last."

She's been doing this. Referencing her departure from Fableview once her birthday passes in November.

It's frustrating me that she can't see the solution yet. But I trust that she will.

On the floor, Anya outdances *everyone*. When my feet start to hurt or I need to get a drink of water, Anya continues dancing. When Kyle Holtzenberg starts asking who will let him lift them, she offers herself up as the first person to be hoisted above the crowd.

She smiles at everyone so much I think her mouth must be sore, because it's never gotten this much use. I'd say I don't recognize her, but that wouldn't be true—I see her better than ever. The light behind all that darkness has been waiting to be let out, and tonight she's like a star, bright and inextinguishable.

"We need to start bringing her water," Grace says, catching me watching. "This pace is unsustainable."

"You're right," I say. "Let's put together a little food plate too."

We head to the snack table, scanning the various treats for

things we think would appeal to our dancing queen. Most of the baked goods are homemade, brought in by members of the Fableview Fall Planning Committee. They're all labeled, but so many people have stampeded through the table that some of the labels are too water stained or crumpled to read.

Grace throws together a plate, and I get the waters. When we return to the gym, Anya is exactly where we left her, spinning and clapping in the middle of the floor.

"Doyle!" Grace calls out. "It's time for you to eat."

"I'm dancing!" Anya responds.

Grace gives me a look. "Does she think I can't see that?" She shoves her way back through the crowd, still holding the plate of treats. I follow with the waters, taking a sip of my own along the way.

"Take a bite," Grace says, pushing the plate toward Anya.

Anya almost keeps going, but she seems to think better of it, stopping and grabbing the first thing she sees—a cookie she shoves into her mouth in one piece. "This is good," she says, pointing to her mouth in shock.

"What is it?"

"Oatmeal chocolate chip."

"My favorite." Grace grabs the next cookie on the plate and takes a bite.

For a while, the four of us dance. It's the most fun I've had in months. Maybe ever. There is no one asking anything of me. No pressure to keep this whole dance running. It's just my girl-friend, my best friend, her love interest, and me, spinning to-gether under a disco ball, not a single care in the world.

Midway through one of our favorite songs, Grace's expression shifts. It's not her usual Grace drama either. It's something . . .

flatter, somehow. She says nothing, just heads toward the gym exit, her pace increasing with every step.

It's strange enough that even Anya stops moving. "What was that about?"

I want to say something like "You know Grace," but this isn't like Grace at all. Grace doesn't walk away from things without explanation. She likes to talk more than anyone I know, make a big splashy scene of an exit wherever she can.

Anya senses this too, and we both leave the dance floor.

The hallway outside the gym is empty. Only a few lights are on, just enough to make sure it's not pitch-dark. The moonlight does more heavy lifting, turning everything from the lockers to the linoleum into the dusty navy of night.

"Grace!" I call out, spotting her near the now-unattended sign-in table.

She doesn't turn back. She keeps walking, but her pace slows, until suddenly, she stops, slumping to the ground.

"*Almonds*," Anya and I say in unison, running to Grace.

Her lips have already swelled to double their size, and her eyes are glossy and bright. A million thoughts crowd my head. She carries an EpiPen in her purse. That must be what she came into the hallway to get. The baggage check is just beyond the sign-in table.

"Which bag did you bring?" I ask.

She points toward the closet where they've stored the bags and jackets, misunderstanding my question. There's no time to overthink. I'm sure whatever bag Grace has brought will be immediately identifiable as hers. I'll have to use my best friend intuition to figure it out.

Except the closet is locked.

"I think I can break it," Anya says. She puts her hands over the lock, closing her eyes in the way I now recognize as magical. The lock melts under her touch, returning to the liquid version of whatever metal formed it. There's no time to ask her how she's undone it or wonder about this development.

There's no time for anything.

I leap inside, tearing through piles of coats and purses, searching for one that looks like Grace's. *I'm taking too long*, I think, my panic increasing. I need to be calmer.

Anya joins me, plucking through the piles I've haphazardly created. "It probably has a reptile on it," she says. "She has a snake clip in her hair tonight."

She's right. She's always right.

"Good call."

It narrows our search, hones our focus. "Go back and keep an eye on Grace," I say. "I'll keep looking."

I don't know how long I search or how much time passes. How much time we have at all. Grace hasn't had a severe reaction since we were really young. I'm fighting not to recall the horrible way she gasped for breath, writhing on the ground as our third-grade teacher stabbed her leg with an EpiPen. Weeks later we found out that Joey Longardi had snuck an almond into Grace's lunch "just to see what would happen."

As soon as I find this pen, I will have to channel my bravery instead of crumbling under the pressure and fear. It's what Grace would do for me. She'd jab a million EpiPens into my leg if necessary.

There are too many bags and coats in here. Or maybe my mind is too scattered. A better use of my time would be to alert an adult. Call 911. Every second is precious.

When I return to the front hall, Grace is still slumped over, and Anya's right beside her, kneeling. "Grace, please. Stay with me. It'll just be a second. Please."

For the first time, I understand Julia. How she'd asked Anya to heal her grandfather. Anya had told her she couldn't. That's not what her magic is for.

I could never ask her that. We have medicine for this. We just have to get it.

I run past the two of them to go back into the gym for an adult, or a phone. Anything. My heels clank against the ground so hard that it shakes my teeth.

Suddenly Grace lets out a loud, gasping breath, stopping me in my tracks. I look back, afraid this is one of those last-breath-of-life things. But Grace is sitting up. Groggy, but alert.

"I didn't fix it all the way," Anya whispers.

Everything is so frantic that it takes me a second to understand.

She's used her magic.

"We still need to call an ambulance. Her airways should be open enough for her to make it to a hospital." She brushes Grace's hair off her forehead. "You're okay. I've got you."

There isn't time to thank Anya. To tell her that was reckless. Any of it. I rush into the gym, letting everyone know what's happened.

The ambulance arrives. The Fall Ball comes to a pause as we watch Grace getting wheeled off on a stretcher. I answer questions for adults, telling everyone that Grace ate a cookie with almonds and went into anaphylactic shock. Then I lie just as smoothly, saying Anya was able to get Grace's EpiPen, buying her enough time to get to the hospital to recover.

No one here knows what Anya did. Only her and me.

Still, her mood is dark. Part of me wishes Grace could see it, because this is *real* brooding.

"You saved her," I remind Anya, hoping to lift her spirits.

"I broke the rules," she tells me back.

"But no one knows that."

"I know it. And so do you. And somehow, I know my family does too."

I don't ask questions, because I can tell she doesn't want to hear them. Once the ambulance has left, the dance resumes, but no one's heart is in it.

"I have to go," Anya says, sulking off into the night.

# 32

# ANYA

At least my last night as a witch was memorable. That's what I
tell myself on the drive home, replaying the Fall Ball in its en-
tirety, trying to memorize each moment so it can keep me company in my new, powerless life. Darcy smiling at me in her dress.
Dancing for hours. Saving Grace.

It was all worth it.

Every last second.

Mom, Dad, and Cal are all sitting on the porch when I park
the Volkswagen in the driveway. I appreciate the fact that they
aren't waiting to do this, not making me suffer through small
talk before sharing the bad news. It's a mercy that isn't lost on
me. They know this will be hard, and they don't want to prolong
it either.

My mom, typically so bright, wears her closest impression of
a frown. Cal scowls as she always does. And Dad is Dad.

"I know," I say, picking up the hem of my dress so it doesn't
get ruined by the wet grass. I'd like to save this too. Maybe I can

put it on sometimes as a sad memento. Like a funeral dress. The last relic of my life of joy.

"Doyle witches don't mess with the natural order of human life," Aunt Cal says anyway, despite my generous lead-up.

I don't bother saying that I know. It's the first thing any of us learn when we start training. It's been repeated by every mentor I've ever had. It's what I would've explained to Julia, if she'd ever actually wanted to listen. For most of my family, it's the one rule they set for me at all, knowing my power might be strong enough to actually do it. Only Cal has given me another—her rule about not having a romantic relationship with a protector.

"I'd say I'm sorry, but I don't regret it," I tell my family. "I will gladly give my powers up if it means that Grace is okay."

All I can hope for is that stripping my powers doesn't hurt. My mind wanders anyway, envisioning the coven putting their hands on my head like some kind of magical electric chair. Or maybe it's slower. Maybe it's a detox that takes days, and I'll be stuck in a room all alone until my powers run dry.

"You did the right thing," Cal says.

Her words startle me out of my imagined nightmare. She's not frowning, not any more than usual. If anything, she looks . . . proud.

"This isn't the same as an old man who was dying of cancer," she continues. "If anything, the way you saved your friend will help you with your initiation. You've shown a willingness to aid your community. To use your magic around here for good."

It's not the mention of the initiation that catches me off guard. It's calling Grace my friend. When it was Darcy in that position, it never fit. Kyle Holtzenberg is a good guy, but I wouldn't call us friends. With Grace, it's easy. Obvious.

I saved her for a lot of reasons. She's a good person. She ate that cookie because she thought it was the same kind as mine, and I felt bad about that. I saved her because she didn't deserve to *die* at the Fall Ball.

But I also saved her because she was—no, is—my friend.

Grace Manalo is my friend.

"How did you know I did it?" I ask.

"It was the vision I had when your parents came," Cal tells me. "I saw you holding her. Darcy watching. At the time, I hadn't seen you with that girl before, so I knew you were still keeping something from us. I also knew you needed to be in charge of your own decisions. Telling you would just confuse you, make you think you should do something else."

Aunt Cal opens her front door. It feels symbolic, this moment, ushering me into the house. It's a gesture of kindness as much as it is a confirmation: *You are welcome here. You belong to us. You've always belonged to us.*

"So I'm not, like . . . banned from joining?" I ask, still afraid to move. "I interfered with death."

"I think we'd all quit the coven if that was what made it so you couldn't be one of us," Mom says, walking down the steps. Meeting me where I am, then helping me move forward.

Inside the house, Aunt Cal gives me tea. Dad rubs my shoulder.

"I'm sorry, I don't want to push my luck, but did I or did I not break the number one rule?" I ask.

"Personally I'd say what you did was more of a helpful boost for the paramedics than a complete changing of her fate. I think it's a gray area," Cal says.

She's lying. Stern, serious Aunt Cal is lying.

For me.

"For safety's sake, we will keep it as our little secret," she continues. "Just don't bring it up around your Uncle Edward."

This gets a snicker out of Mom and Cal. He's their younger brother and, judging by my time with him, kind of a prick.

"Okay," I say, taking a sip of the concoction Cal's made. It's perfect, all the herbs she's chosen designed to steady my nerves.

I thought this would be my undoing, but instead, it's given me the strength to do what's needed.

I'm ready to choose my protector.

# Halloween

# 33

# DARCY

When I come down the stairs into the art shop the afternoon of Halloween, the last thing I expect to see is my parents putting the finishing touches on Anya's costume.

"You're a *witch*," I say with delight.

My mom's putting a red lip on Anya as my dad lowers the signature pointed hat onto her head.

"I hear I'm supposed to sprinkle another year of good fortune atop Fableview today," she tells me.

My mom heads into the supply closet, then pops back out with the glitter vial.

"You know, that myth is true," Dad tells Anya. "It's based on your grandmother."

"She could fly on a broomstick?" Anya asks, sounding, for once, as skeptical as me.

"I don't think so. But it felt like it," my mom tells her. "She was a special woman. You have her eyes, you know."

Anya's eyes fill with tears, quick and unexpected.

"She always wanted to keep this town safe," Mom continues. "And she wanted to make it as magical as possible. She's the one who came up with half the things we do throughout the month. And now you and Darcy have worked so hard to make them even better." Mom hands Anya the glitter, completing the look. "To sprinkle," she says with a wink.

"We heard about the haunted house," Dad says. "You really shook the Holtzenbergs up. They don't want our job anymore." He's grinning big, hugging the straps of his *Ghostbusters* costume.

"Good," Anya says to him conspiratorially.

"We just need to find someone we like who can take the reins for us someday," Mom says. It's hard not to hear it as one last little dig about my planned departure. But it's also true. They're in their sixties now. They deserve to retire. They deserve nights in front of the TV falling asleep to old movies. *Someone* has to take their job.

"We'll find the right person," I tell them. "But we have to leave. Grace wants us to get the best candy, and you know how fast that goes around here."

Anya and I head onto the boulevard.

"No, no," I tell Anya when she tries to go into one of the shops for candy. "Don't be fooled. They're only giving out minis. Witches of Fableview hands out *stickers*." I don't hide my disgust. "We have to hit your aunt's neighborhood. Those are the real candy dealers."

We make our way over there, passing kids and classmates alike, everyone crunching autumn leaves and breathing in the crisp air while dressed up in their Halloween finest—witches, goblins, Marvel characters. They've all got a place in Fableview.

Anya and I have three plastic jack-o'-lantern canisters to fill, one for each of us and a third for Grace, who's still recovering at home, devastated about losing the chance to debut the lizard costume she's been working on for years. She insisted I wear it instead, and so, in her honor, I've traded in my fairy wings for scales.

"I love that no one here is too old for this," I tell Anya as we pass full-grown adults collecting candy.

"I didn't used to feel that way," she says. "I used to think this was all kind of ridiculous. And I see now what I've been missing out on."

"I think having literal witches in town helps make it magical," I say back.

"I don't know. What I did with that lock at the Fall Ball might've been a YouTube tutorial."

We laugh.

Anya hasn't told her family yet about the way her powers have shifted. That, in addition to healing things, she can also *break* them.

"Very cute," I say, kissing her quickly.

"I love you," she blurts.

This grinds me to a stop halfway up Mr. Breck's driveway. He may be negligent when it comes to checking his parade ropes, but his wife passes out full-size packs of Starburst every year.

"Everything is just so much better when you're around," she continues. "This holiday, my powers. You make me like these things about myself that used to scare me. And I just . . . I know it's probably too early for me to tell you I love you, but I do. I really do. I love everything about you."

I grab her hands. Our candy buckets crowd the moment,

but even that is perfect. It's a little silly, a little ridiculous. I'm in Grace's lizard costume, after all. Anya is a real witch dressed as my family's impression of a witch. But it's completely, totally us.

"I always think about that first day I met you," I tell her. "How badly I wanted to know you. Because I think even then I could tell that to be seen by you would be the greatest gift I could ever receive. And it is. You always recognize the parts of me that everyone else overlooks. You can pick my art out of a lineup every time. You hear the fear inside all my performed confidence. And I know that you see me. Because I can see you too. It's like we have on these glasses that only we share, showing us what no one else notices. I love being in that world with you. It's my favorite place to be. Because you're my favorite person. Ever. Of all time."

"I love you," she says again.

I kiss her once, quick. "Please!" I protest. "Let me say it back!" She settles again, her foot doing an adorable shuffle of impatience. "I love you, Anya Doyle."

A car honks as we kiss. The honking continues long enough for us to break apart. Without even looking, I know who it is.

Anya seems to as well, because she keeps her eyes on me as she says, "I think Kyle has powers. Like, I really believe he can teleport."

"I kind of agree," I tell her.

"Sorry to interrupt," Kyle says, leaning out his car window. He's dressed as a medieval knight. His little brother, Karl, waving from the passenger seat, is also a knight. "Just wanted you to know we got the Lego castle."

"Thank you so much!" Karl says, full of a bright sincerity that makes both Anya and I melt. "I really love it!"

In the end, we didn't give Kyle money. Instead we found the Lego castle in the toy shop down the street from Pam's Paints, and we split the cost down the middle.

"We're gonna start building it tonight if you guys wanna come over and help," Kyle tells us.

"Maybe," Anya answers. "We have to stop by Grace's first."

Kyle presses a hand to his heart. "Tell her I'm thinking of her. I dedicated my shoulder workout to her this morning."

"We'll text you," I say, waving him off to go teleport his ridiculousness elsewhere. "I'm glad you love it," I tell Karl.

"It's amazing!" he calls out again as they drive off.

"What a little sweetie." I turn back to Anya. "What was I saying? Oh yeah, I was telling you I love you."

"I think you already said it," she says.

"That doesn't mean I'm *done* saying it."

"Well, we should probably continue our proclamations on foot. You've got me worried we won't get enough of the good stuff for Grace."

We continue trick-or-treating. And it's so silly, but it's also the best, getting to do this with her.

This is the magic I've never failed to believe in—the kind that only Halloween can bring, innocent and hopeful. A wonder that never goes out of fashion. At least, not in a town like ours. And I know that if I get the chance to leave for college next year, it's Fableview that's made me ready. Because that's what the spirit of this holiday does. It inspires us to try on different lives as often as possible. To have the courage to become someone new.

# 34

# ANYA

Mrs. Manalo wraps me in the biggest hug I've ever had, tears springing to her eyes.

"Thank you," she whispers over and over.

I don't know what story Grace told her—the EpiPen one or the truth. It doesn't matter. This town would protect me either way, but no one would take more care with that truth than a Manalo. I get the distinct impression that every single one of them would personally fistfight my Uncle Edward if he somehow found out and caused trouble over it.

It's Maddie who interrupts us, tugging on my cloak to get my attention. She's dressed again as a manananggal, wearing the wings I mended for her. It's much gorier this time. The fake blood is all over, and there are pool noodles attached to her that have been painted to look like intestines.

"You're a witch!" she says, pointing to my hat.

"I am," I tell her.

"I knew it," she says.

"Come in, come in." Mrs. Manalo beckons. "Grace is upstairs in her room. She will be so glad to see you both."

Maddie attempts to follow us up the stairs, but Mrs. Manalo stops her. Maddie starts to cry, and I turn back. "We'll come down soon, I promise. Then we can hang out," I say.

When we get to Grace's room, she's under the covers, wearing a green silk pajama set and one of those headbands designed to hold your hair back for makeup. It's the first time I've ever seen her face bare, and she looks so young—she *is* so young—that it dissolves any last lingering regret I have about breaking my family's magic. She has so much ahead of her.

"You guys are late," she says.

"We have a good reason, I promise," Darcy tells her, handing over our carefully sourced candy bucket.

Grace combs through it like she's TSA at an airport and this item has been plucked for further examination. She picks out the full-size Starburst, and I expect her to smile, pleased, but she remains stoic. "Very good. Thank you." She sets the candy bucket on her nightstand, then folds her hands together over her comforter. "Well . . ." she says expectantly.

I shoot a look at Darcy. Maybe this is a bad idea. Maybe we need to wait until Grace feels all the way better. But Darcy's almost laughing. There's something here that I don't understand, haven't all the way worked out.

I decide to press on, ignoring my rising panic. "How are you feeling?" I ask as a warm-up.

It's also a valid question. She's been through quite the ordeal.

Grace doesn't answer for a long while, locking eyes with me the way she used to when she told me she was watching me. When I was "sinister." I roll backward through the past few hours. Have I wronged Darcy? Was it too much when I told Parker Holt to take care of Grace? What has her so upset?

Finally Grace breaks, pointing to the box in my hand.

"Come on!" she says. "I'm waiting for you to ask me! We can do the how-are-yous afterward!"

"You know?" I say, looking again at Darcy, who now has her hands up in surrender.

"I didn't tell her! You know I'd never do that."

It's true. She wouldn't.

Helpless, I fumble with the box, all my plans thrown off by this development. Grace lets out another sigh, one of her throatiest, most theatrical groans, and opens her nightstand. The two walkies sit side by side. She hands one to me, then keeps the other for herself. "Doyle, this is Manalo. Do you copy?"

"Manalo, this is Doyle. I copy."

"I figured it out because I'm brilliant. Over," she says.

When I don't lift the walkie to my hand, prepared to compliment her in person, she nudges me with her leg under the comforter until I lift the walkie to my mouth. "I see," I tell her. "I should've figured."

"Yes," she responds. "Okay, you can put it down now."

I set the walkie on the edge of her bed, and I hand her the box. She tears it open without ceremony, so fast that I don't have a chance to tell the story about why I picked it. Not that she needs to hear it anyway. She's always been ahead of me, so it's probably right this way.

"A lizard pin!" she says with her usual delight, clapping as she attaches it to her pajamas. "It's perfect. Great touch." She winks at Darcy, knowing that bringing a ceremonial gift was her idea.

"Grace," I say, all my plans out the window. "Will you be my protector?"

She throws the covers off her bed like she's Charlie's grandpa in the super super-old version of *Willy Wonka & the Chocolate Factory*, ready to skip her way to the candy factory. She even strikes a pose, one hand behind her head, her opposite foot popped out.

"Of course I will," she says. "Who could do it better?"

"No one," I tell her. And that's the truth. There is no one who would look out for me the way Grace Manalo would.

When she's done posing, she gives me a hug. "Seriously," she says. "This is a really cool honor. I can't believe I get to help the *real* witches of Fableview. It's all I've ever wanted. Having powers would stress me out, so getting to help other people who have them is exactly the right role for me. Thank you for seeing that." She pulls back. "And thank you for being my friend."

"Thank you for being *my* friend," I say, insistent. Those pesky tears of mine spring up again.

"*Awww,*" Grace and Darcy say in unison, squeezing me from either side.

"Let it out, Doyle," Grace tells me. "It's healthy."

No matter what comes next, I know I have them both to lean on. I owe all this to Darcy for giving me a chance. For believing in me when no one else did. And it's a little bit like magic, really, how one person can come along and change your whole entire life.

# A Few Months Later

# 35

# DARCY

I'm the first to reach the ancient computer we keep in the back office.

"How old is this thing?" Anya asks, watching me boot it up.

"You know, Anya, technology used to have personality," Dad tells her, coming up beside me to run a finger over the monitor's teal outer shell, lifting a layer of dust in the process.

I glance back over my shoulder to say, "It's from 2001."

This gets a genuine gasp out of Anya.

Mom laughs, setting down a tray of cookies she's baked for us all. "He talks a big game, but this thing doesn't have any of its original components other than the monitor. You can't believe how much he's spent on keeping it running."

Dad shrugs. "What can I say? Some old things are worth keeping around."

Even though this is ridiculous, I wouldn't have it any other way. I could check my email on my phone, but that's not the point. The spectacle is the point. And getting on my dad's early-2000s computer is the only way I'd ever want to find out if any of my chosen colleges have accepted me.

The doorbell chimes.

"That must be Grace," Anya says, springing up to answer it.

She disappears from the back office, leaving me alone with my parents. "Thank you," I tell them again, "for letting me do this."

Mom kisses my forehead. "You did this on your own. You deserve the credit."

"Our brilliant baby girl," Dad adds.

"No matter what happens, we're really proud of you." Mom switches to hugging me sideways, in the same spot she always takes when we're on the couch.

"We're the proudest that two parents could ever be," Dad says.

It wouldn't be a moment with them without this kind of talk. I don't even mind it. If I'm honest, I might have set them up for it, needing one last boost before everything changes in a permanent way. Before college becomes not just a dream but a reality.

When Anya returns, Grace is with her, carrying a handful of balloons. "I know we don't know for sure, but let's call this wishful thinking," she says in explanation. "And we can pop them if you don't get in. It will be really satisfying. I brought baseball bats too, in case we want to break stuff."

Grace has decided she doesn't want to go to college. I admire her for it the same way I admire everything else about her. She loves Fableview the way my parents do, and she doesn't have any interest in seeing what's outside of this place, not even when I've pleaded with her to look at some of the schools I've applied to. She knows herself. She always has. And that's why she's my best friend.

With all my loved ones gathered together, my nerves kick into high gear. I might fail in front of them. All the struggle—the fights and the back-and-forth that got me to this place—may have been for nothing. I might be destined to be a Fableview lifer after all.

I sit in front of the monitor and go over the game plan. "I'm gonna start with my top choice," I say. "If it's bad news, we're not dwelling, okay? We still have four more to check. And if I get denied from all five, we're stomping on the balloons Grace brought."

"Exactly," she says solemnly.

It takes a second to navigate the login, my hands shaking so hard that I can't get my password right.

Everyone arcs around me. Anya puts a supportive hand on my shoulder. Her touch, so assured, gives me an unexpected wave of confidence. Maybe it's her magic. Her healing. Or maybe it's just her, the way she can slow down my racing mind, holding me to the present as only she can. It gets so quiet that every click I make echoes, sharp and loud as a stapler on paper.

And then I see it.

One word.

*Congratulations!*

"You did it," Anya says softly, right as Grace screams. She pops off a confetti cannon. My parents erupt in applause.

It's Anya I hold first, wrapping my arms around her and resting my head against her shoulder. "I knew it," she's telling me. "I'm so proud of you."

And she *did* know it. Through every wavering doubt, she's been there with encouragement. In exchange, I've been helping her understand the other side of her magic. Now that she's an official member of her coven, she's finally told everyone in her family about her new ability to "unmend" things, as she likes to say.

They've been excited by the development. Thrilled to learn that magic can evolve the same way everything else does. She and I have both shattered our old lives into a thousand pieces together, and now here we stand in what we've built atop them.

"I'm going to college," I say. The giddiness kicks in.

Grace and I spin each other. "You're going to college, bitch!" she says. Then she remembers my parents are in the room, and she gives them the same speech she once gave Anya, about how "bitch" is a term of endearment.

Unlike Anya, my parents need to hear it. They nod along, confused but forced to accept it. Then they smother me in kisses and hugs and tears. We return to the computer, where I check the other schools. I get into two more, wait-listed for one, and rejected from the last, but it doesn't dim the shine of this. Nothing could.

When we exit the office, another surprise awaits. The shop is filled with people—Piper, Kyle. The Doyles. The owners of the shops along the street. Our Fableview Fall Planning Committee.

They cheer as I walk through. I turn to my parents, expecting to find that they're responsible for this. But they point to Anya.

"What if I hadn't gotten into any of them?" I ask.

"Impossible," she says, grinning as she squeezes my hand. "But we'd have had a rage party instead. Grace really did bring bats." Then she looks out over the crowd. "I hope this is a good group. I handpicked who got invited."

"It's perfect," I tell her.

My parents take out the mic we use for our biggest events, encouraging me to give an impromptu speech. Unprepared, I attempt to give my thanks. Somehow it evolves into this sobbing, impassioned speech about everything Fableview has given me. How much I'm going to miss this place next year. How nowhere else can ever compare.

When I'm done, there isn't a dry eye in the house. Not my mom. Not Anya. Not even Aunt Cal, who has been the hardest one to crack in a town full of particularly tough nuts.

I shove the mic back into my dad's hand, afraid I've brought the mood down with my dramatic speech. "Tell them something happy," I say. "Please."

He recovers as only he can, that customer service brightness always right within reach. "Thanks for celebrating our baby girl," he says to the crowd. "She wants me to share something happy, and I think I have just the news. We're thrilled to announce who will be taking over the shop for us when we retire."

This sends a ripple of surprise through the audience. Including me. We haven't discussed this in weeks. It's been my last loose thread, the nagging worry that I've been concerned I'll carry all throughout college.

My mom joins Dad at the mic, putting a hand around his shoulder in support.

"We don't know anyone with more commitment, enthusiasm, and dedication than this person," he continues. "And they're young, which certainly helps two old farts like us. My bones crack every time I walk up and down these stairs. This young sprite will have no problem. Not for a few decades, at least."

My mom gives him a nudge, returning him to the point.

"The next owner of Pam's Paints and the future leader of the

Fableview Fall Planning Committee is none other than Grace Manalo!"

Grace runs up to the mic like she's been waiting for this. And in so many ways, she has. It makes perfect sense. Grace knows the town's secrets, and she guards them with ferocity. She has no plans to leave. How could it ever be anyone but her?

"Thank you," she says, hugging my dad. "I didn't know we were doing this today, and I want to be sure we don't take too much shine away from my best friend, so I'll keep this brief. I can't wait to keep the magic alive every fall, and I will do everything I can to preserve the traditions of our strange little town. Thank you! And congrats to Darcy!"

She blows me a kiss, flitting off into the crowd to receive her appropriate congratulations.

Anya's hand finds mine again.

"That fits," she says.

"It does," I tell her.

And then we face each other, and the rest of the world falls away. It's just her and me inside the art shop, the same way all this started.

"I love you," I say.

"I love you right back," she tells me.

She rests her forehead on mine.

I don't know what will happen in the fall when I leave for college. But I know we'll figure it out somehow, because that's what we do together. We solve what no one else can.

Broken, fixed, or anything in between, we fit.

# ACKNOWLEDGMENTS

First off, this book would not exist without my editor, Hannah Hill, whose seed of inspiration grew into what we now know as Fableview. Hannah, I'm honored you gave me the chance to create my very own cozy Halloween town, and I am very glad we got to make book magic here together. I also owe so much to my interim editor, Arianne Lewin, who brought fantastic insight and boundless enthusiasm to this project, helping me polish this book into the sweet, sapphic YA romance of my dreams.

Huge thank-yous to Makena Cioni, Kaitlyn San Miguel, Colleen Fellingham, Alison Kolani, and the rest of the team at Delacorte Romance for welcoming me with open arms. I've wanted to return to YA for years, and you've all made it a complete delight.

To say I am gobsmacked by this book's deliciously witchy and perfect cover would be an understatement. Thank you to Brittany Keller for the stunning illustration and to designers Casey Moses and Ken Crossland for bringing the whole package to life.

Taylor Haggerty—my agent of ten years this year!—thank you for letting me press my foot as hard as I can on the gas pedal. You've made my writing career a reality, and I am so grateful for the enduring strength of our partnership. Jasmine Brown, Melanie Figueroa, and the rest of the Root Literary team, I remain in awe of the way you champion authors with such enthusiasm and passion.

Every story I write is a reflection and celebration of the love I feel around me. I am so lucky to have family and friends who still get excited about my books. You know who you are, and I hope you spend a lifetime uncovering all the ways I've tucked the magic of our bonds into the corners of every story I write.

Finally, to my readers, it's an endless honor to have you here. I hope this book feels like all your favorite Halloween memories brought back to life. Never lose your wonder and whimsy.

**Return to Fableview
for Piper and Ivy's story . . .**

I PUT A *Spell* ON YOU

**COMING SPRING 2027**

**BRIDGET MORRISSEY** lives in Los Angeles but hails from Oak Forest, Illinois. When she's not writing, she can be found cradling one of her cats like a baby or headlining concerts in her living room. Bridget is the author of novels for teens and adults, including *What You Left Me*, *When the Light Went Out*, *Love Scenes*, *A Thousand Miles*, *That Summer Feeling*, *Anywhere You Go*, and *This Will Be Fun* (written as E. B. Asher with Emily Wibberley and Austin Siegemund-Broka).

**bridgetjmorrissey.com** 📷

2 04

# In the charming town of Fableview, every day is Halloween.

**DARCY KELLER**, resident ray of sunshine and town spirit princess, loves every moment of Fableview's fall festivities. But she's also *really* ready to leave for college next year, even though her parents expect her to stay and take over their Halloween empire.

Enter brooding new girl Anya Doyle, a real-life witch and *almost* a full member of her coven. To be initiated, she has to choose a mortal ally to act as her "protector." But having moved around so much, Anya is completely friendless. So she does what any self-respecting teenage almost-witch would do—she lies and tells her coven that her secret crush, Darcy, is willing to do the job.

The solution? Work together, of course. The girls agree to help each other out, attending everything from a costume parade to a pumpkin patch party to an apple bobbing contest together. But with Anya's magical powers and Darcy's future independence on the line, the last thing they need is the added complication of pesky feelings . . .

"Swoony, witchy, and sweet. . . .
The perfect read for rom-com lovers everywhere!"
**—JENNIFER DUGAN,**
**author of *Some Girls Do***

GetUnderlined.com | @GetUnderlined

Cover art © 2025 by Brittany Keller
Cover design by Casey Moses

Manufactured in the United States of America
Also available as an ebook and on audio

**DELACORTE ROMANCE ❤ NEW YORK**

US **$12.99** / **$17.99** CAN
ISBN 978-0-593-89843-7

5 1 2 9 9

9 780593 898437